MERCUTIO

by

J.I. DAVENPORT

For Wendy,

So sorry you missed it.

All my love.

I

Queen Mab

THE moon shone high above the streets of Verona, yellow as a gold ducat. Along the dark and cobbled streets, those cowardly minions of the night that we call shadows trembled at the coming of flames and a riot of voices. The stroll to the Palazzo Capuleti was all mirth and merriment, and Mercutio seemed gay as ever as he regaled his company of friends, maskers and torch-bearers with tales of fairies and talk of dreams; but, behind his filigree eye-mask adorned with silver wings, Mercutio was afraid.

The fear had come with the setting of the sun. He had been dressing in his newest silk and velvet when he'd noticed a tightness in his shoulders, a brittleness to his fingers. He'd fumbled with his cap and broken a feather. Then, he'd dropped a bottle of ambergris tonic. Since when had he become a *nervous* person? What did he think was watching him that could see through walls, through roofs, through flesh and bone? When he was little, his alchemist father had explained to him the power and influence of the stars. If it was so, then Mercutio was certain some fateful star had appeared that night to set grave events in motion: a great cataclysm from which he would not be spared. Searching the dusky sky from his casement window, he'd seen nothing but moon and clouds; but apprehension continued to roil in the pit of his stomach, and two cups of wine had not settled it.

As he'd sat waiting for the knock on his front door, he'd begun to fear that his dread would give way to mania, as it had sometimes before. What if he lost control, and on so star-crossed a night? Surely, he would wake tomorrow in his grave.

A third cup of wine had ensured a great show of gaiety when his friends came to collect him. It had been his idea to go to the summer ball in the first place. His kinship with the Prince of Verona guaranteed him an invitation to every social event of the year; but it was the need of his dearest friend that had prompted him to take a band of merry Montecchis with him. Romeo Montecchi was forever suffering for love. His starry eyes had a habit of finding the most beautiful-yet-unattainable maidens in the land. This time, they had fixed on Rosalina the Fair, a radiant flower of the noble House of Capuleti. Chief amongst the lady's virtues was her chastity, however, and she shunned all overtures of love, preferring her prayer book to the sonnets of Dante and Petrarch. As usual, Mercutio had conspired with Romeo's cousin, Benvolio, to ease his aching heart, and their plan tonight was to smuggle him into the Capulets' masquerade, where he might see *la bella* Rosalina outshone by the other young beauties of Verona. This meant a venture into enemy territory, though: for the Capuleti hated the Montecchi.

Their grudge was such an ancient one that none lived who knew its origin, though colourful rumours abounded like wildflowers. The Montecchi had once betrayed the Capuleti to the Pope. The Capuleti had betrayed the Montecchi to the Holy Roman Emperor. A dragon had once granted them three wishes to be shared equally, but one house had cheated the other out of the third wish. Which house cheated depended, of course, on who was telling the tale. A Capulet was likely to tell you that an ancestor of his had once taken a Montecchi to wife, and that she had used witchcraft to enslave his soul. A Montecchi would claim that it was *his* forebear, in fact, who had taken a Capulet

3

bride, and that she had confessed on their wedding night to having been deflowered already by her father and twelve brothers: for the Capuleti held to heathen practices to ensure their daughters' firstborns were always of the "purest" blood.

Who knew how much truth, if any, was in these tales; and, more to the point, who gave a fuck after all these years? as Mercutio often asserted.

Romeo was in a tenacious melancholy that night. Though he had dressed handsomely for the ball — and Romeo could never help but be handsome — he remained in no mood to go. Rather than pressing him to cheer up — as Benvolio had been doing all day — Mercutio knew a better strategy was to stir up a whirlwind of gaiety around him, in which he would gradually allow himself to be swept away.

'What does a yellow moon portend, I wonder?' said Baldassarre, Romeo's young servant-boy.

'Good fortune, surely,' Mercutio replied. 'You are to be swamped in gold and blondes, tonight — mark my words.'

Mercutio capered along the cobbles leading into the Piazza delle Erbe, the market square that had once served as Verona's forum in the marble days of Caesar and Augustus. In the shadow

of the Lamberti tower, he swirled his cloak around as his following came to the last lines of a bawdy ballad.

'Did I tell you I met an Englishman, yesterday?' he asked
them abruptly.

'No, I think you did not,' Benvolio replied.

'You do not think I met him, or that I did not tell you? 'Tis
no matter — do not interrupt! The man I speak of was a playwright, and he was passing through our city on a pilgrimage to
Rome. I could not understand his name, but it reminded me
somewhat of *Guglielmo*. Anyway, "Guglielmo" the playwright
told me the most charming folk tale from his homeland. It concerned a minuscule fairy queen, no bigger than the heliotrope set
in the ring on my finger.'

'A sizeable lady, then!' his torch-bearer jested.

'Not big enough for you, Gaspare,' Mercutio retorted. 'For I
have seen the size of your favourite tavern-wench! But this
queen of whom I speak is a dainty thing, and so small that she
may ride her chariot up the noses of men as they sleep.'

'Why should she do that?' asked Benvolio.

Once Mercutio had ascertained that all ears were his, he

said, 'So that she may enter their heads and deliver their dreams. Not just any dreams, either, but those of fulfilling your heart's desires. So, tell me, good gentlemen, what dreams would Queen Mab deliver unto you?'

Mercutio flapped his cloak like fairy wings as his companions began to talk excitedly of riches and beautiful women. Mountains of gold. Oceans of jewels. Rivers of silk. Fields of flowers, waiting to be plucked. Islands of nymphs, dying to be fucked.

'Sounds about enough for me!' said Gaspare.

'I would dream I had a *magnificent* face,' said Vitale Lessini, 'and one that was all my own. For I would establish myself far better as a credible tragedian if I did not have to share my face, as well as the stage, with my dear brother.'

'You didn't share it,' Ariello Lessini replied, 'I stole it from you.'

'You did not!'

'I did, too! You never share anything, so I steal them.'

'Are you calling my brother a thief?'

'Are you calling your brother a liar?'

6

'I call you a whoreson!'

'Then, I must defend our mother's honour!'

While the Lessini twins leapt into each other's arms to wrestle it out, Mercutio manoeuvred himself near to Romeo and listened with one ear as Baldassarre spoke to him.

'If Mab enchanted your sleep, sir,' the boy asked, 'what would you dream of?'

Romeo sighed. 'That I held the heart of she whom I love in the palm of my hand. For it is more precious than any ruby known to man, and more impervious than the adamant-stone.'

'Good Lord,' Mercutio cried. 'I knew that you loved the lady, but not that you also wished her violence!' He mimed cutting out his own heart and holding it aloft, still beating.

Romeo shrugged off the jest and returned the question. 'And you, Baldassarre?'

'I, sir? I would dream that I was Prince of Verona — nay, King of Italy — and that I was waited on by a hundred serving-men and women in my palace!'

The boy blushed at the hoots and cheers his confession received. Looking to shift the attention elsewhere, he turned to his

7

fellow servant and hastily asked, 'Abramo, what say you?'

'My dream would see me join Melania di Villafranca in her bathtub,' Abramo replied, to raucous approval.

'You'd have to wait in line,' Benvolio muttered so that none would hear. He knew he'd not been entirely successful, however, when Mercutio turned to him suddenly, his brow lifted in astonishment. Why would the gentle Benvolio impugn the honour of Melania di Villafranca? And why so furtively? Clearly, the matter warranted some enquiries; but Benvolio pre-empted him:

'What of you, teller of tales?' he asked quickly. 'What would you see in your dreams?'

Romeo.

Mercutio's foreboding was stirring again. The shadows on the street seemed to have found their nerve at last: for they loomed at him from all directions now. Something was going to happen tonight that would seal his fate. It was too much to know such a thing — no mortal should have to see his coming doom — and, in answer to the question, Mercutio began to rail against Mab's cruelty. She was a gnat! A gadfly to the human spirit! For what kind of malevolent sprite would give a man dreams of that which he could never hope to have in his waking life? Surely

8

such torment, night upon night, would drive even the sanest man to insanity; the strongest to self-destruction.

The words poured from his mouth, but they came from a place beyond his control. Drowning in his own despair, he realised it was the mania taking hold, and that he could not stop it. Suddenly, the piazza seemed impossibly vast and empty, as though he were completely alone. He looked to the sky and trembled: for there was a colossal archer in that starlit realm, training an arrow of fire on him. Tonight, the string would be loosed, and the fatal shot would course its way to his heart with inescapable accuracy. When it would strike, he did not know, but he knew now that his life was near done.

Snatching off his mask, he opened his mouth to scream at the heavens — to deafen the gods with his rage and sorrow — but, as he took the huge intake of breath, a hand lighted on his shoulder. Romeo was by his side, calm and concerned, and it took the breath from him.

'Peace, Mercutio, peace,' he urged softly, cupping his face with cool hands. 'What do you rail at? Fairies? Dreams? Nothing.'

He was right. Dreams were but the children of an idle brain.

9

Yet, there was a thinness to Romeo's smile, a waver in his gaze that looked like doubt. Mercutio realised then that he must feel the very same presentiment, and that he too was afraid.

'Come, friends,' said Benvolio. 'We tarry here so long that the ball will be done before we arrive. Baldassarre, strike us a merry beat!'

The boy began to play his hand drum, and the Lessini twins burst into song to spur them onwards.

Mercutio happily yielded, but as he glanced back, his eyes caught Romeo's like magnetite. A thousand words passed between them in an instant, though Mercutio did not know what they were. He saw fear, beauty, sadness and love, all in a single gaze; but did he see the faintest reflection of what, in that moment, filled his own heart? Did Romeo feel the same?

He was glad not to have to think on it for the next few hours. Parties had become his favourite diversion from the woes of his life: be it a wine stain on his favourite doublet, a debt festering with impatient creditors, or the fact that he was hopelessly in love with his best friend. The prospect of imminent drinking, dancing and mischief-making seemed reason enough to set all else aside, for now, and be merry.

10

'Now, then,' he said, throwing his arm around Benvolio as they walked, 'what is it that *you* dream of, my little friend? Plucking the Fair Rose for yourself, perhaps? Hush, now — do not speak! For we approach the Palazzo Capuleti, and they will know from your rustic tongue that you are a mountain-dwelling Montecchi!'

II

Men's Eyes Were Made to Look, and Let Them Gaze

MERCUTIO, Romeo and Benvolio bade their attendants farewell outside the Palazzo Capuleti, giving them coins to spend in the nearby tavern until the hour they were needed to light them home. Vitale and Ariello hurried on ahead, hoping to slip amongst the troupe of hired entertainers before they were missed.

The footmen at the gates admitted them all without prejudice: for they recognised the Prince's nephew by the winged mask he was so fond of wearing.

'Welcome, *signor* Mercutio,' they greeted him, but he put his finger to his lips.

'There is no Mercutio, tonight, my friends,' he replied, 'only

Mercury.'

Navigating the glowing halls of the palazzo, Mercutio led the way through the crowd of ladies and gentlemen flocking towards the ballroom. At the entrance stood the master of the house, *signor* Orlando Capuleti, welcoming the multitude with the kind of gusto that could be heard across the Alps.

Benvolio started fiddling with his mask. The sight and sound of the Capulets' paterfamilias was enough to make his hands falter; but it was the man at *signor* Orlando's side who called to mind the danger they courted in coming here. Tensions between the Houses of Montecchi and Capuleti were volatile. Only that morning, a petty quarrel between their servants had erupted into a full-blown riot, beatings and stabbings and all. In the aftermath, Abramo had sworn by the Blessed Saint Zita that the instigator had been a brash, red-headed fellow by the name of Sansone, a footman from the Palazzo Capuleti.

As they drew near their host, Benvolio saw that very same Sansone attending *signor* Orlando with a torch, his hair slicked back with bacon grease. Benvolio dreaded to think how the Capulets would react should he and Romeo be discovered in their midst, but he feared another brawl: Verona's sovereign ruler,

Prince Escalo, had finally come to the end of his patience with them, and had decreed death to the next Montecchi or Capulet to breach the peace.

Mercutio, however, was perfectly content to believe that a pair of pseudonyms was all that was needed to avert a lynching. 'Fear not, "Benigno",' he whispered. 'I shall speak to old Orlando and his knave while you and "Romolo" slip past. Go, get you a drink and enjoy yourselves! Ah, good evening, *signor* Capuleti.'

'Welcome, good Mercury,' their host replied. 'What tidings bring you from the realm of the gods?'

'War! Famine! Floods! Plague! Earthquakes! Madness! Death! That is why Jove advises we drink tonight like there is no tomorrow: for, chances are, there won't be!'

'Wise counsel. I, too, then, shall drink tonight as Jove prescribes — and He can answer to my lady in the morning!'

'Is your good wife within?' Mercutio enquired, but he did not listen to the answer. He had seen Sansone's eyes following the two youths who stole past without a word. 'You, there!' he exclaimed, pulling off his cloak and flinging it over the footman's head. 'Be a good fellow and take care of that for me,

14

would you?'

Shrieking, Sansone fought to free himself of the garment whilst keeping it from the flames of his torch. By the time he had managed it, Mercutio had wished *signor* Orlando a very good evening and hurried on.

'Did you see that, master?' Sansone cried. 'He tried to kill me!' Receiving no word of comfort, he dashed the velvet cloak to the floor, for which he received a clip round the head.

It was always difficult to ignore the moment Mercutio entered a room. The people of Verona had mostly given up trying. *Best let him have his moment, or he may never quieten down!*

'*Buona sera*, one and all!' he cried, bursting into the ball-room in a flourish of canary-yellow silk. A sea of faces turned his way, and he greeted them with a frivolous bow.

No one could deny that he at least gave them something to look at. His doublet was undeniably as bright and gay as a canary, heavily brocaded with leaves and flowers in white and gold thread. His fancy sleeves were puffed at the shoulders and slashed to reveal naughty glimpses of violet satin. Tight, parti-coloured hose flaunted his legs to their utmost shapeliness. His head was topped with a cap of outrageous purple velvet, matching the vibrant gloves adorning his hands.

Velvet gloves in summer? Only Mercutio!

Yes, indeed, he was fair, and it went beyond his sun-blond hair. There was a natural symmetry to his face and body that was nothing short of statuesque. The length of his neck, the width of his shoulders, the curve of his jaw — even the shape of his ears — all were as exquisitely formed as if sculpted by an artist. Yet, it was simply the way he was born. His eyes mirrored the sky: azure by day, sapphire by night. While his lips were not the fullest, they were of the finest shape and definition thanks to their deep crimson colour. He would never deny that Romeo had always been the one with the lips.

Whether Mercutio was vain or not was a difficult question to answer. You had to understand him. He often complained, himself, of the young men he saw preening about the city, obsessed with image and etiquette. He certainly did not count himself amongst that pride of peacocks. He was too much the rule breaker and rebel at heart, delighting in the controversy and outrage he excited as much as the envy and admiration. He was beautiful and fashionable and a living satire of men's vanity.

16

While others might boast of the height of their brows or the shapeliness of their calves, Mercutio was more likely to pull down his hose and extol the peachiness of his buttocks. In fact, the habit had earned him the epithet *il Callipigio*, which alluded to sculptures of the goddess Aphrodite that had been worshipped by the ancients for their "lovely buttocks".

But he would not subject the Capulets to such behaviour, tonight — not while he was this sober, at any rate. He smiled and offered pert pleasantries to those he passed, all the while looking out for his Montecchi companions. Yet, it proved impossible to find two shadows in a room filled with light, so he decided to make for the wine as expediently as possible.

The Capulets' ballroom was truly a palace of bright night. The walls had been draped with reams of gold brocade, reflecting the abundant candlelight and amplifying the brightness. Pillars and archways hung with garlands of evergreen shrubs and citrus fruits. The banqueting table overflowed with platters of quail eggs and sliced truffles and summer berries, set amongst grand arrangements of lilies and roses. The kegs of wine were all but in sight —

'There you are, young rogue,' said a steely voice at Mercu-

17

tio's side, and he found himself snared arm-in-arm with *donna* Salvatrice, the elderly widow of the lamented statesman, Vitruvio Panzavecchia.

'Good evening, *madonna* Panzavecchia,' Mercutio replied gaily.

'Good evening, indeed. But where, pray, is your good wife?'

'Perhaps the wine and excitement has left *madonna* a trifle confused. Else she would surely remember that I am not married.'

'I know it, and your mother tells me you are most dismissive of the candidates presented to you. Porzia Mancini, I believe, is the latest to meet with your disdain.'

''Tis the name, *Porzia*. Always puts me in mind of "porkers". Not very promising, is it?'

'The Mancini are one of the oldest and richest families in Italy, with strongholds in Rome and the kingdom of Sicily. Your uncle, the Prince, should like nothing better than to ally with so powerful a family — particularly now that that red-haired devil of Milan, Gian Galeazzo Visconti, has his greedy eye on our city. A marriage would be the ideal way to seal such an alliance; yet, you see fit to turn your nose up at it! Then, there was the Doge of Venice and the hand of his lovely niece, which would have certainly secured us a better trade deal —'

'Lady, you are a better politician than your late husband! I prithee, bother my cousin with these concerns. *He* is still a bachelor, and near ten years my senior.'

'Count Paride tells me of an engagement that will shortly put his bachelorhood to an end, saints be praised. His mother can sleep easily now, but what of yours? It would be a tragedy for *donna* Marzia to never know the joy of grandmotherhood.'

''Tis like motherhood, surely? Only grander!'

'And, since the Bishop has declined to annul your brother's marriage to that wretched Paduan girl, you are now your family's last hope. It is every man's duty to ensure that his branch of the family tree continues to bear fruit. For Jesu himself did curse a fig tree for bearing naught but leaves.'

'Why, *madonna* Panzavecchia! How careless of me to forget that *you* are now in the market for a new husband. But if all this fecund and fruity talk is to sow the seed of your own proposal, why not just come out with it?'

19

'Enough cheek, now! Give me an answer: will you marry or won't you?'

'I will! I will marry you, mistress of my heart!' Mercutio declared loudly enough to ensure an audience of amused onlookers. 'Get me to a friar and I'll be thine, if thou'll be mine!'

'Enough,' snapped the dowager. 'I see you are every bit as incorrigible as your mother describes. Well, I leave you to the mercy of Saint Augustine, for I wash my hands of you.'

'That is what I have always admired most about you, *madonna*: your pleasing standards of hygiene.'

'Here comes your cousin. Perhaps *he* can talk some sense into you.'

'I wouldn't count on it. Ah, Cousin! How fine you look, tonight. Is that for me?' and before Count Paride could answer, Mercutio had commandeered his goblet of wine.

'In truth, Cousin, I need no wine this night to drown my heart in joy,' Paride declared generously.

'Why so?' Mercutio asked blandly. 'Oh, yes, the virago in the wimple mentioned something about an engagement?'

''Tis true, Cousin. By this very year's end, I shall be called

20

"Husband". By this time next year, I'll likely be called "Father".'

'You intend to leave your bride for the priesthood?'

'Nay, Cousin, I mean —'

'Well, who is the lucky contessa-to-be? One of our *la bellas*? Or have *you* been poached by the Mancini?'

'I … cannot say, at present. Her father asks me to defer my suit for two more summers, so that I may first win her heart. But I *know* that tonight is my test. Here, amongst the brightest beauties of Verona, I am observed so that the constancy of my heart may be assessed. When her father sees that my eyes are for his daughter alone, he shall not delay a week!'

'Perhaps you could win the gentleman over by showing him your cock?'

Paride turned white as chalk.

'Well, he has won you prizes, has he not?' Mercutio reminded him. 'How is King Chanticleer?'

'Dead as a doornail, I'm afraid. Fowl pox. Took out the whole coop. Didn't have the heart to eat him, so he's been stuffed. Still brings a tear to my eye, actually …'

21

In truth, Mercutio had stopped listening; but his ears pricked at the mention of his brother's name.

'How fares Valentino?' Paride enquired. 'I had hoped to see him here, tonight.'

'You would have been wiser to ask, "How fares the Veil of Saint Veronica?",' Mercutio replied, 'for, then, I could have answered that it has been seen more often than my brother! In short, he has never been the social type, so a summer ball would be the last place I'd expect to find him.'

''Tis a pity. I heard his marriage has been no bed of roses. But what of you? Rumour has it you got on splendidly with the Doge's niece at the *Carnevale*. Might Verona soon have cause for another celebration?'

Mercutio was about to reply with an emphatic *No*, but his attention strayed again as he spotted a slender youth loitering behind a pillar, still fiddling with his mask.

'I am overjoyed to hear of your engagement, Cousin,' he professed rapidly. 'For it is every man's duty to ensure that his branch of the family tree continues to bare his plums, and all that. And so, good Paride, let us go forth and multiply!' With that, he clapped his cousin on the back and dashed off.

'Prepare to die, Montecchi!' he said once he'd crept close enough to Benvolio so that only he would hear. However, he did not reckon on having to catch his friend by the arm to stop him bolting like a wild colt.

'Peace! Peace! 'Tis only me: your wicked friend, Mercury.'

'Thank Heavens,' said Benvolio, relief outweighing his annoyance. 'I thought you were Pluto!'

'Where is your cousin, "Petrarch"? Gone to steal a glimpse of his beloved "Laura"?'

'That cannot be. For there dances the lady who has his heart, but Romeo's not here ...'

'So he isn't. And so she is. Oh, how fine *la bella* Rosalina looks tonight in her gold and coral silk. See how her fair hair doth gleam golden by candlelight. Did the Blessed Virgin's halo ever shine so brightly? And, lo! How gaily her grey eyes do flash with every graceful turn. But what is that I spy in her delicate hand? Why, 'tis a rose, as white as the fingers that doth hold it!'

'She is more beautiful than a saint,' Benvolio professed.

'Then, why not ask her to dance?'

'I ... cannot.'

23

'Why, may one ask? Was it not you who urged Romeo, earlier, to tread at least one measure, when he swore his soul was too heavy to lift a foot? Yet, I'll wager you have not moved one toe in time to this music! So, I say again: why not ask the fair lady to dance?'

'I ... err ... she is engaged at present with Count Anselmo.'

'Oh, 'tis not an engagement, only a *saltarello*. I am sure the Winter Rose would rather lift her feet with a lithe, hazel-eyed youth than an old, grey Count. Should I ask her to dance for you, perhaps? Mercury can be your messenger —'

'Mercury mistakes himself for Cupid. Oh, look — I think I see Romeo!'

Mercutio could not catch his friend's arm again, and found himself alone once more.

Romeo. Everything else in Mercutio's life was a case of out of sight, out of mind. Except Romeo. Where on earth was he now, if not haunting the steps of Fair Rosalina?

III

Borrow Cupid's Wings and Soar with Them Above a Common Bound

As Mercutio finally achieved his goal of reaching the wine, he felt the room rustle like a field of grass. There was a rising murmur of voices, and he looked back to the entrance. A young woman had appeared on the threshold, dressed in an off-the-shoulder gown of blood-red damask. She wore a gold crown studded with rubies, about which her black hair was arranged in twists and braids that tumbled down her back in a cascade of darkness. Her eyes were framed with a mask of seashells and shining nacre. Above her tight bodice, her alabaster breast twinkled with a lavish necklace of pearls. Yet, all these adornments paled in comparison to the luscious beauty smouldering beneath them: potent, erotic, uncommon amongst the gentle ladies of her class. As she sauntered through the crowd, a young man in the musicians' corner struck up a sensual melody on his mandolin: his own secret serenade to her.

'*La bella* Melania,' Mercutio greeted her, 'as radiant as the Evening Star. I think I've forgotten what you look like by daylight!'

Of all his female friends, Melania di Villafranca was Mercutio's favourite. Whilst the other girls he knew strove endlessly to blanch the darkness from their hair with lye and lemon juice, Melania's was unashamedly as black as ebony and gleamed like a river of satin. Her eyes, too, were dark, but deceptively so: they revealed their midnight blueness only to those fortunate enough to come close to her. Counted among the great beauties of Verona, she was one of an elite group of young ladies who were afforded the title "*la bella*" in everyday conversation. She was also called Melania *Verticordia* — the Changer of Hearts — an epithet she shared with only one other woman in the universe, who happened to be a goddess.

'Did you bribe that mandolinist?' Mercutio teased.

'Giustino Capuleti and I are old friends,' Melania replied

with a smile. 'We shared the same music tutor when we were children, so we often had chance to play together.'

'What sweet music you must have made, fiddling and strumming away. Did he give you the pearl necklace?'

'No, this was a gift from an old flame. The one I told you bore a passing resemblance to you, in fact.'

'Are you sure you did not meet this fellow in your dreams? For I know of no man living worthy of such comparison.'

'If I were skilled to pull gems from my dreams, Mercutio, I would stand here the Queen of Sheba.'

'So, that is *your* heart's desire ...'

'Your meaning?'

'Meaning? You've come to expect meaning from what I say? Poor girl. You're in need of wine! What do you say? A drink? A dance?'

'Aye, to all.'

'Do not say that too loudly, my dear. When a beautiful woman stands in a public place and declares "Aye, to all" she is liable for a stampede!'

Mercutio led Melania back to the wine and filled two goblets from an open keg. Passing her the first, he muttered, 'Lo!
We are watched by our hostess ...'

Melania glanced discreetly in the direction he'd indicated.
After a moment, she whispered, 'See the way she looks at me?
She despises me.'

Though her tone was subtle, Mercutio did not miss the un-
derlying relish.

'Narcisa Capuleti despises any woman who dares to be more
beautiful than she,' he replied philosophically. 'To this day, it is a
rare occurrence for her.'

'Even if she is the wrong side of thirty,' Melania retorted.
'Yet, Saint Rosalina manages to avoid her aunt's disfavour.'

'Yes, but family is different. And Rosalina's beauty is less —
predatory? — than yours.'

Melania laughed with such pleasure that she placed a hand
on Mercutio's arm to steady herself. The delightful sound roused
the attention of several young men nearby, and, soon enough,
one had plucked up the courage to present himself.

'Good evening, *la bella*,' he said, his voice faltering. 'Would you care to dance with me?'

'It is most kind of you to ask —' she began unfavourably.

'Oh, do not disappoint him, *la bella*,' Mercutio intervened, whispering, 'for I hear that Lucio Faetini is better on his feet than off them.'

'In that case, I will dance with you, *signore*,' said Melania. 'After Mercutio.'

She took Mercutio by the hand — and he, likewise, took Lucio — and they moved to the centre of the ballroom, where rows of colourful ladies and gentlemen hopped, skipped and wheeled around in time to a lively tune. They joined the steps of the *saltarello* with courtly grace; but it was not long before mischief occurred. A glint in Mercutio's eye, a curve of Melania's lips; then, as the flutes began to rise, she braced her hands on his shoulders and he lifted her into the air and swung her around. Gasps and cries peppered the air around them, and many watched with open mouths as the Changer of Hearts took flight once, twice, three times more.

'Ah, *madonna* Panzavecchia,' *signor* Capuleti began, 'I hope you are enjoying —'

'Orlando Capuleti,' she cut him off, 'do you intend to stand there and allow such obscenity to go on, under your roof?'

'Bless my soul! What obscenity can you mean? Oh, I see! Some new form of galliard they picked up in Venice, I'll wager.'

'We are not in Venice, thank God, *signore*.'

'They are but children, *madonna*, showing off for our amusement, no doubt. Surely, no harm can be done when none is meant.'

'I see,' the dowager said finally. 'Then, I must bid you a goodnight. I pray you, think on this pearl, if you can: "Women may fall when there's no strength in man."'

With that, Salvatrice Panzavecchia quit the ball.

'By Jove!' said Tolomeo Capuleti, Orlando's aged uncle. 'I do hope the young lady does not fall.'

'Mercutio's as strong as any young gallant of Verona,' Orlando reassured him. 'What danger is there of him dropping her?'

'I've heard it said that young Mercutio is as audacious among maidens as a lion among lambs,' Uncle Tolomeo said with a naughty chuckle.

'Where on God's earth did you hear that?' Narcisa Capuleti scoffed.

By now, Melania had taken Lucio's hand, and Mercutio was seeking to quit the dance floor and refill his goblet. He managed but three paces before his way was blocked by two women.

'Just a moment, *signore*,' said the elder, who he recognised as Fiorenza degli Albizzi, the Florentine wife of old Uncle Tolomeo. 'You have not yet danced with my daughter,' she charged him. 'No, no, do not try to refuse. There are not enough young men to go round. Why every man here has brought his wife, sisters, nieces and daughters with him, I do not know!'

Mercutio was about to offer a crude witticism, but he was cut off by the lady's dumpy daughter.

'I shall dance with you, *signore*,' Cesarina Capuleti asserted, 'but you may not lift *me* off the ground.'

'True,' Mercutio agreed, 'for, despite Vitruvius's theory that gravity is not dependent on a substance's weight, I fear that, in this case, gravity would most certainly be against us.'

Cesarina gasped in horror, but a gesture from her mother si-

31

lenced her as the musicians began to play *presto*.

'Ah, *la moresca*,' Mercutio noted. 'Very well, *signorina*, let us tread a measure.'

They joined the other ladies and gentlemen preparing to dance the moresca, a jolly pantomime inspired by the Moors of North Africa.

Led by the Lessini twins, the troupe of entertainers came frolicking into the ballroom, dressed in stylised Moorish costumes and wielding prop swords. Circulating among the guests, they handed out colourful scarves, feathers, tambourines, and strings of bells that everyone tied to their wrists. The ladies then gathered in the centre of the room and began dipping in time with the music, while the men formed a wide circle around them, flicking their wrist-bells in unison.

'I must confess, my wrists have not known such exertion since I was thirteen!' Mercutio declared. 'I daresay you are in far better practice, Cousin.'

'Yes, indeed,' Count Paride replied absently, '... I mean, no!'

Mercutio was not the only fellow in the circle who could not contain his enthusiasm and began following the ladies' choreography, raising his arms in graceful forms and hopping and twirling on the spot.

Such levity lifted the mood to new heights of gaiety, and, by the time the dancers had paired up, everyone was laughing without a care in the world.

IV

Blind Is His Love, and Best Befits the Dark

THE hour was fast approaching midnight. The moresca had come to a jubilant end, and the guests were leaving the ballroom, ushered along by the actors and jugglers, while the musicians played them a cheerful goodnight.

Stepping out into the night air, Mercutio removed his cap and felt a sweet relief. A cool breeze soothed his hot skin, caressing his damp hair like the breath of a loving mother. It was too warm to don his velvet cloak, so he bundled it under his arm — noting it had been brushed since he'd last seen it — and looked about the crowded forecourt.

The Lessini twins were amusing the pretty sisters of Count Anselmo, walking on their hands alongside them. Lucio Faetini was chatting pleasantly with the nieces of *signor* Piacenzo, though Mercutio knew the sweat on Lucio's brow belonged to none but *la bella* Melania. He did not so much see as *hear* Cesarina Capuleti somewhere in the throng, complaining to her mother that Mercutio Marchesino was the only man in all Verona who felt the need to sing along as he danced!

He was about to answer her complaint when a hand seized his arm. Before he knew who had hold of him, he was being pulled away, towards a wall of ivy. A wooden door appeared among the leaves, and, when he was on the other side of it, he found himself gazing into the hazel eyes of Benvolio.

'Zounds, man! I thought I was about to get lucky,' Mercutio jested. 'Did you find your errant cousin, then?'

'I have found him and lost him again,' Benvolio answered.

'How have you managed that?'

'Romeo is more slippery than an eel, tonight. What? Why does that tickle you? Mercutio, be serious! I found Romeo soon after I left you, but he seemed so … *queer.* No longer listless or melancholy, but agitated — excited, even — though, still, he would confide nothing. But his eyes were so … *changed.* So … I cannot describe it, but you would understand if you'd seen him.

35

He looked as if he'd been enchanted. Bewitched! His pupils were so enlarged — so gaping — as to turn his blue eyes black, like those who've drunk of nightshade.' A sudden fear came to him. 'You do not suppose the Capulets have *poisoned* him?'

'I would not fear it,' Mercutio reassured him. 'Though I imagine a "belladonna" is the likeliest cause. Perhaps the Winter Rose has given him some sign that his hopes are not entirely in vain. I wonder what it might have been ... A smile? A wink? A flash of nipple? That would have certainly gingered him up!'

'As to that, I cannot say,' Benvolio replied, once he'd won the battle to keep his face straight. 'In truth, I was keen that we should leave. There were eyes in that ballroom that watched us too long. That man in the cat mask looked ready to pounce! I'd just persuaded Romeo to leave with me when we were intercepted by *signor* Capuleti, urging us to stay. I gave him our excuses while Romeo went on; then, I tried to catch him up, but he was far ahead of me. I almost called out his name, till I remembered where we are.'

'That is why I advised you call him "Romolo" this night,' Mercutio chided. 'For there are but two Romeos in all Verona — and the other is a gravedigger! Rarer still are Benvolios: for there's but one of those in all Italy.'

'And but one Mercutio in all the world,' Benvolio recited, as though he'd heard it said a hundred times.

'Too kind! Now, "Benigno", why have you dragged me out here? Is this not the way to the Capulets' orchard? Has Romeo gone cherry picking at this hour?'

'He must have gone this way,' Benvolio explained. 'I came out of the palazzo straight after him, but he was nowhere to be seen. I could not fathom it until I heard the sound of a latch, which I traced to the ivy. He must have slipped through that door, quicker than a fox, and is somewhere along the lane ahead.'

'And I suppose we cannot just leave him here, like Daniel in a den of lions, but must deliver him safely back to the milky bosom of his mother?'

Benvolio nodded timidly.

Mercutio skipped and hummed the tune to the moresca as they began down the cobbled lane, which skirted the perimeter of the Capuleti estate. The golden moon hung low in the sky now, preparing to take its leave of the night. The air was sweet with the scent of July roses, blooming in the walled gardens. Though in the heart of the city, the Capulets had spared no expense in making it possible to believe one was strolling through a country idyll.

'There,' Benvolio said suddenly. 'Is that not him, atop that wall?'

'I see no one,' was Mercutio's reply.

'He has leapt down into the orchard. But I am certain I recognised his colours. In truth, Mercutio, did you see any other man this night whose clothes were particoloured in black and blue?'

'Verily, I did not,' Mercutio replied thoughtfully. 'I saw a man in black … and I saw a man in blue. I saw a man in blue and black, but not in black and blue.'

'*Cousin*,' Benvolio called as Mercutio danced about, singing:

> '*I saw a man in black*!
> *I saw a man in blue*!
> *I saw a man in blue and black*,

But ne'er in black and blue!'

'Mercutio, as you are a true friend, help me to call him,' Benvolio entreated.

'Very well,' he agreed, and cleared his throat. Affecting a sweet, *falsetto* voice, he called:

'O, Romeo! Romeo! Wherefore art thou, Romeo? 'Tis your lady love, Rosalina … (Hark, Benvolio! Did you hear him come running? No?) Ahem! I say, 'tis *Rosalina* of the House Capuleti. Hoped thou to find thy way to my bedchamber over yonder wall? Saucy knave, thou art out of luck! For I do not bed by fruity orchards, but in a cell nearest the chapel. 'Tis a cold cell — nay, *frigid* be the word — and ne'er visited by man.'

'Mercutio, you go too far,' Benvolio cautioned. 'If he hears you, you will anger him.'

'Anger him? 'Tis not the spleen that governs his body this night, but another organ far more inclined to be sanguine. But why do you hide from *us*, dear Romeo? Are we no longer to be trusted? Is it that you suspect one of us of having his own designs on your Fair Rose? You see, Benvolio, *you* are the cause of this distemper.'

39

'I am innocent, I swear!' Benvolio protested.

'We believe you, don't we, Romeo?' Mercutio cupped his ear for a reply. None came. 'The ape is deaf! Man must have lived without ears when he dwelt in that Garden of Paradise. It is often said forbidden fruits are sweetest; but what of the serpent, Romeo? If it should begin to rear, I pray you, do not be tempted to pet its head: for it will spit in your eye as rudely as a cobra!'

'We call in vain,' said Benvolio. 'Hark! I hear our men in the street, come to light us home.'

'Goodnight, my Romeo,' Mercutio called. 'I go to my bed of straw. Clearly, there is no room for us in your bed of grass. Benvolio, shall we go?'

'Aye. There's little point seeking one who means not to be found.'

Mercutio threw his arm around his deflated friend, and they continued on to the end of the lane, where a door to the street awaited them. Hearing soft voices behind them, Mercutio peered over his shoulder.

'Lo! Here comes the Changer of Hearts and her dumpy maidservant.'

'I shall to Abramo and the others,' Benvolio said hastily. 'Goodnight, good Mercutio!'

'Come to mine for breakfast, tomorrow,' Mercutio called after him. 'And bring that haughty cousin of yours — if he should ever be found again!'

'Aye to that,' Benvolio replied over his shoulder.

'Well met by moonlight, fair Melania,' Mercutio greeted the cloaked woman approaching. 'And I say not goodnight, but good morning: for we have entered the witching hour, by my reckoning. Speaking of which, does that not mean your companion has somewhere to be? A black mass or a virgin sacrifice, perhaps? Though, where they find their sacrifices these days is beyond me!'

Melania's attendant looked as though his words had made her ill. 'I see *signor* Mercutio still prefers the sound of his own voice to all others,' she said, crossing herself against his impiety.

'Mother, is that you?' he retorted. 'Oh, pardon me, Mother. It is so dark, I mistook you for a vegetable in a dress.'

'Thank you, Carmiana,' Melania interjected. 'You may leave me now.'

'What, with *him*?' the older woman protested, but a sweet smile from her mistress was enough to placate her. 'Yes, *signorina*,' she said grudgingly, and curtseyed before departing.

'Your dumpling's well trained,' Mercutio noted.

'Ha! She curtseys and calls me *signorina* only when we're in public,' Melania replied. 'At home, she bosses me about worse than my mother.'

Mercutio laughed sceptically, and Melania slipped her arm through his as they walked.

'So, what brings you this way?' he asked. 'Come to smell the roses? Sample the fruits? Catch a spot of music, perhaps?'

'I cannot imagine what you mean,' Melania replied coyly. 'I was following you, actually, in hope that you would lead me to some grand amusement. So, the question is, what were *you* doing out here, all alone with that mousy friend of yours?'

'We were seeking that other friend of mine: the one who is more fox than mouse. He came this way pursuing some folly or other, and sprang over that wall, there, like a monkey!'

'What, *that* wall? Come, let me show you something ...'

Melania led Mercutio to where a great mass of wild roses

grew over the top of the orchard wall and hung down like a curtain. It was a wonder the Capulets had not had it cut down, though Mercutio supposed they thought the same as he: that it possessed a certain rustic charm. He watched as Melania reached for one of the roses — its petals as red as her sleeve — and lifted it to her nose. A gentle sigh; then, she pulled the briar to which the bloom belonged, and the curtain was drawn a little to one side.

'Look …' she whispered, and Mercutio leaned in.

'Another hidden door …' he marvelled. 'These Capulets are a sneaky bunch!'

'I do not suppose it has been opened in decades. The lock has rusted shut, see? But, if you stand in the doorway, you can peek through the cracks in the wood.'

Not asking her how she was so familiar with the Capuleti estate, Mercutio slipped behind the curtain and into the fragrant darkness.

'Mind the thorns, my dear,' he cautioned, holding the briars back for her. 'That's one prick that is never welcome!'

The door in the orchard wall looked very old indeed, its lock

43

and hinges weeping with years of rust, its panels warped and splintering. Side by side, they peered through the largest gaps they could find, but the base of the wild rosebush grew so thickly on the other side that it was near impossible to see anything. Yet, the moonlight played its part, and soon Melania whispered:

'I see someone, I think. A boy …'

'Does he wear black and blue?'

'I cannot tell. It is too dark …'

A wind rustled through the roses, and Mercutio caught the soft murmur of voices.

'Do you hear that?' he asked presently.

Melania concentrated for a moment and then nodded. 'Let's listen.'

V

Such Sweet Sorrow

Y EARS of joy were spent in minutes, leaving none to cushion the days to come.

Mercutio and Melania kept as still as stone effigies as
Romeo came hurrying back to the orchard wall. They held their
breath as he climbed over their heads, caring nothing for thorny
briars, and hopped down in front of them. With a great cry of
joy, he raced off down the lane, stumbling and laughing as he
went.

Mercutio watched his love disappear into the night, a cold
tear tracing its way down his cheek.

'You have to hand it to him,' said Melania, 'when it comes
to wooing, your friend's second to none. Will his inheritance

come with a title?'

Mercutio shook his head.

'Shame.'

In the silence that followed, Melania sensed the notes of a mandolin, calling her to a secluded arbour somewhere.

'Well,' she said presently, 'I think I'd best be on my way. As you said, the hour has grown so late, it is now early. Why, Mercutio! I did not take *you* for a romantic,' and she wiped his tear away with a graceful thumb. Picking a crimson petal from his hair, she kissed his cheek and departed.

Alone, Mercutio wiped his eyes on his sleeve and sniffled. The beautiful words he'd heard exchanged in the orchard had moved him to tears; but they had also broken his heart. He had seen Romeo fall in love a hundred times before, and had always been there to pick him up when love knocked him down. But, to-night, he knew he'd witnessed something more. Something momentous. The girl on the balcony had not only professed to love Romeo, but had expressed it with all the passion and poetry that was characteristic of the man himself. She had matched him, rhyme for rhyme and simile for simile, and Romeo had been overwhelmed by the kindred nature of their souls. So much so that he had sworn to marry her. Tomorrow!

It wasn't as though she was the first to return his affections. Mercutio recalled a comely baker's daughter who'd been all too eager to exchange vows of everlasting love with Romeo; but their romance had fizzled out soon after the heatwave that year had given way to a drizzly September. Either that, or Romeo had already fallen for Bianca Vespeti — Mercutio couldn't remember which — but that was the way it always went. Until now.

Jaw clenched, he peered through the crack in the door on Melania's side. Through the briars, he spied the moonlit balcony and a window beside, flickering with the light of a solitary candle within …

There she was — a dainty silhouette — twirling about the room in her nightgown. Mercutio was sure she was humming — the moresca tune, perhaps — the notes coming from her throat as light and free as a nightingale's. He watched the delicate shadow settle onto her bed and lean in to the candle. With a gentle puff, she vanished into darkness.

Who on earth was she? Not Rosalina Capuleti, that was for sure.

Mercutio left the Capuleti estate a ghost. Pulled by the unconscious forces of habit, he followed the narrow streets leading back to the Piazza Erbe, wondering if his body was still behind the curtain of roses, slumped against the orchard door. He did not know where he was going — only that he could not bear to go home to the little house he rented alone. He'd rather wander the streets till dawn.

If only he had left with Benvolio. He wished he could go to him now, but he knew his friend would be tucked up in bed already — sleep and peace prevailing on him as on a child half his age — and Mercutio would not rob him of his sweet dreams.

Coming to the piazza, he was roused from his inner world by music. The Lessini brothers and their troupe were still at it, entertaining a small crowd with a folk dance around the Madonna Verona fountain. Mercutio knew the steps well enough.

VI

In Bed Asleep, While They Do Dream Things True

ARLIER that year, Mercutio had been invited to dine with Prince Escalo at the Palazzo Grande. Considering the rarity of the honour, Mercutio had suspected some special motive, and, halfway through the roast venison, his uncle informed him of his recent correspondence with the Doge of Venice. In an effort to boost relations between their two states, the Doge had invited a delegation of Veronese nobles to the *Carnevale di Venezia* before Lent, as well as offering to host them at his palace.

Mercutio was only too pleased to accept a place among the delegates; but he was curious to know who else his uncle had nominated.

'Well, your cousin, Paride, was an obvious choice,' said Escalo, 'but he has declined for personal reasons. I shan't bother asking your brother; Valentino has enough on his plate. Claudio Urbana's son, Dionigi, will be going ...'

'Dionigi Urbana?' Mercutio asked in astonishment.

'Not the most savoury choice, I know. But I owe his father's bank some money, and Claudio asked me as a special favour.'

'And, of course, wherever Dionigi goeth, so goeth that giddy cousin of his.'

'Yes, Arianna Perduti will be accompanying him. I have also selected Bruto Capuleti. The last thing I want is that family rioting because they've been left out! His kinsman, Valenzio Cattanei, should keep him in check. But I'd like to ask if you have any more suggestions. You know Verona's social scene better than I do.'

'Have you considered Romeo and Benvolio Montecchi?' Mercutio asked so eagerly that he nearly choked on a piece of gristle.

'I have,' Escalo replied. 'Mercutio, I seriously doubt their parents would approve their going to a Venetian "bacchanal".

50

The Montecchis are known far and wide for their piety.'

Mercutio could not disagree, but the prospect of embarking on the adventure of a lifetime without his two best friends was bitterly disappointing.

'How about Marcantonio di Villafranca's daughter, Melania?' he suggested.

'*La bella* Verticordia? I'm not sure how wise that would be …'

'Melania is as gracious and charming as she is beautiful, damn her! I'm sure she'd make a good impression on the Venetians.'

'I suppose I cannot argue with that …'

'Then, there's the Lessini brothers. They always lift the spirits of a celebration.'

'No, I cannot countenance sending a pair of *actors* to represent Verona at the Doge's Court. What if they started juggling at the dinner table? Besides, twins are bad luck.'

'They get lucky far too often for that to be true!'

'By the way, I imagine you'll meet the Doge's niece while

you're there …'

'Oh, yes?'

'My envoy tells me she is one of the most celebrated beauties in Venice, not least because she possesses an abundance of the strawberry-blonde hair that has become so synonymous with Venetian beauty. Nerissa Delfini, her name is — though the poets call her Nerissa of Troy.'

'Really?' Mercutio replied blandly. 'I'm sure the classical allusions are more than justified, Uncle, but Nerissa Delfini is of as much interest to me as Helen was to Achilles.'

'Even Achilles understood the importance of marriage and children, *proud* as he was. How else may a man live on once his mortal life is spent?'

'Hmm … A glorious death at a young age? It seemed to work for our friend Achilles!'

Ten days before Lent, the Veronese delegation embarked on the seventy-mile journey to the fabled City of Water. Prince Escalo had arranged for them to travel in a convoy of covered wagons, complete with an escort of armed guards. Sojourning in Vicenza and Padua en route to the coast, they were finally met by the Doge's envoys at the port of Marghera. From there, a state barge — complete with trumpeters — ferried them across a green lagoon to a floating metropolis.

Venice was impossible. An Atlantis of white stone and terra-cotta rising from cyan waters. Sailing into the icy San Marco basin, the Veronese beheld the place that would be their home, its white facade shining on the waterfront. The Palazzo Ducale was not only the majestic residence of the incumbent Doge, but the seat of the Venetian government. Its style exemplified the Gothic Byzantine architecture that peppered the city's melting pot. Above columns and arches of Istrian stone, herringbone brickwork laced its way up to a hipped roof, behind which rose the gilded domes of Saint Mark's Basilica.

The Veronese were greeted at the palace's waterside entrance by the chamberlain, who took them directly to the Great Council chamber, where the Doge and his councillors awaited them. As Prince Escalo's kinsman, it was Mercutio who presented the Doge with the letter of goodwill from his uncle. It was given to the censor to read to the Council, in accordance with the law prohibiting the Doge from having private correspondence with foreign rulers, "lest he become involved in affairs that threaten domestic harmony".

'I quite understand, gentlemen,' Mercutio assured them, 'for my mother often cited that same wisdom when caught reading my father's correspondence!'

It was then Dionigi Urbana's turn to present the Venetians with a chest of gold from his father's bank. Dressed for the occasion in emerald-green samite — denoting his status as one of the banking and merchant class — Dionigi oversaw the gold's handover to the Doge's clerks, who would take it to be paid into the Republic's treasury. However, he and his cousin, Arianna, seemed more interested in the palace's handsome footmen, who they planned to divvy up between them.

With their business concluded, the Veronese took their leave of the Council and rejoined the chamberlain, who gave them a tour of the palace before showing them to their quarters in the luxurious guest apartments. They were to spend their first day in Venice being shown the sights — shipyards, banks, basilicas, and the great *Arsenale* — then, when night fell, they would join the *Carnevale*.

The festivities continued for seven days and nights, and Mercutio relished every moment. From Castello to Santa Croce, every district of the city glittered with the delights of the *Carnevale*. Jugglers and acrobats showcased their skills on each corner, while merry minstrels harped, fiddled and fluted to the stars. Fire breathers lit up the streets like warring dragons. Crowds thronged the public squares to watch the endless plays and pantomimes.

The ceremony in which a bull and twelve pigs were paraded through the streets in wooden castles was the most hilarious thing Mercutio had ever seen — that was, until the animals were ritually slaughtered and distributed to the masses. A sailor told him it was a proud tradition, commemorating the Serene Republic's victory over the Patriarch of Aquileia and his twelve canons in 1162. However, to Mercutio's sensibilities, it was but a grisly remnant of the Dark Ages. Nor was he overly keen on the bull runs held in the perilously narrow streets; but he loved the riotous cart races, on which he bet and won and lost hundreds of ducats. Then, there were the fabulous costume balls, held all over the city in the grandest public buildings. Donning an array of fantastic costumes, Mercutio and his companions strove to visit as many as possible each night — though as soon as the witching hour was upon them, they would quit the masquerades and take to the streets, immersing themselves in the festive anarchy. They revelled till dawn and then slept all day, rising only to prepare for the night to come.

During their time at the palace, they became familiar with the Doge's family. One of the first to greet them had been Michaleto Bevilacqua, the Doge's gregarious nephew. Michaleto was a roguish sort who, despite having a wealthy senator for a father, often found himself short of money and thus obliged to lean on his uncle's generosity. In a bid to curry favour, he had taken it upon himself to befriend the Veronese visitors and serve as their guide and escort. He was also the one to introduce Mercutio to the eligible Nerissa Delfini, who had lately been the subject of a poem entitled 'La Bella Anadyomene' — *The Beauty Rising From the Sea* — a not-so-subtle allusion to the birth of Aphrodite.

'Rising from the sea ...' Mercutio had mused.

'Along with the other whales,' Melania had whispered.

Mardi Gras was soon upon them, and Mercutio had heard that the wildest revels were yet to come. As the sun set over the City of Masks, he and the others gathered in their lounge for wine and baklava before going out. They had saved their fanciest costumes for tonight, and the servants seemed to move about them with added reverence.

Melania had amazed everyone when she'd emerged from her room as the fabled Queen of the Nile. Her white-and-gold samite gown sparkled with a galaxy of beads and gems, each one hand-stitched by her maid, Carmiana, who had also embroidered her sleeves with sacred ibises. Melania had crowned herself with a special headdress plated with gold and lapis lazuli, which her father had commissioned for her from a royal jeweller's in Paris.

Fancying himself as the Great Alexander, Dionigi was strutting around in a white-silk tunic overlaid with golden armour, which helped add some heroic bulk to his scrawny frame. A regal cloak of red-and-gold velvet hung from his shoulders, while a gilded olive wreath nestled proudly on his ashen head.

Judging by Arianna's colourful and highly Asian-looking costume, she had guised herself as Alexander's queen, Roxana of Bactria. She'd been telling anyone who'd listen all about the merchant she'd found in the Rialto marketplace, who had recently travelled the Silk Road to Afghanistan and had sold her a "*salvare camisia*". She had even managed to find a Moorish kitchen maid at the palace, who'd helped her to decorate her hands and feet with henna.

Vitale and Ariello Lessini made an altogether theatrical pair, garbed as court jesters and masked as Sock and Buskin — though they refused to tell who was who or which was which.

Bruto Capuleti had shown arguably less imagination with his fancy dress for Mardi Gras. He sported his gladiator costume — *again* — though a new cloak and an old bronze helmet from the marketplace now made it his "Spartacus" costume.

His cousin, Valenzio, had spurned the heathen past and guised himself in all the chivalry and romance of the Crusades. For this, he had acquired an old shirt of chain mail from an iron-monger, which he wore with leather boots, suede gloves, and a velvet surcoat emblazoned with gold crosses.

Mercutio's costume had been the most interesting acquisition of all. During a rare daytime excursion, he'd been exploring the Rialto when the wares of a Chinese pedlar had caught his eye. In particular, a sleeve of the most unique silk he'd ever seen, pro-truding from a rack of wools and cottons. Bright and glossy, the sleeve was, and brocaded with patterns of fruit — halved peaches, to be exact — which had been rendered so finely that Mercutio remarked on it to the pedlar and asked of its significance.

'In my country, legend of the bitten peach,' the man explained in broken Italian. 'Very old — from before your Christ. Mizi Xia was young courtier of Duke Ling. So handsome, he Duke's favourite companion! One day, they walk together in orchard. Mizi Xia see ripe peach on tree and pick it. Bite it. Most delicious fruit ever tasted! Mizi Xia want to eat all, but he stop and give it to his lord. The other courtiers outraged. Insult Duke Ling with half-eaten fruit! But Duke understand.

'"How sincere is your love for me?" he declare. "You give up your own pleasure so that I may share it!"

'Mizi Xia loved all the more, after. But time pass, looks fade, and Duke cast him aside in end. Yet, ancient poet says "love of the bitten peach never dies".'

Mercutio bought the peach robe for a hundred ducats, along with silk boots and pantaloons figured with peach blossoms, a black courtier's cap, and a mask of Ming porcelain. He doubted they had ever belonged to an actual courtier; more likely they'd been made to portray Mizi Xia on stage.

And so, the night of Mardi Gras had been his turn to play the lover of Duke Ling, though he did not share the pedlar's story with his companions. He was simply a handsome prince of the Chinese court, and his ensemble attracted many compliments. The brocading was so detailed that he and his admirers were still discovering new images: narcissi on his collar; a goldfish nibbling at a peach on his sleeve; two peacocks entwining his legs; a red chrysanthemum blooming over his heart.

'You have a cock on your back,' Arianna pointed out.

'He should be so lucky!' the Lessini brothers chorused.

Soon, a tuneless trumpeting heralded the coming of Michaleto, and he appeared in the doorway, a conch shell pressed to his lips. His costume put Mercutio in mind of wily Odysseus: all sea-green samite and brown leather, with a cloak of gold netting. With him came his cousin, Nerissa, looking every inch the Nereid in a gown of foamy-blue damask, dripping with strings of pearls and coral. Trailing them was a sleepy page boy, carrying an inlaid chest.

'Greetings, my Veronese friends,' Michaleto proclaimed. 'May we join you for a drink?'

'Certainly,' Mercutio answered. 'You are now the guests of your guests, and we can hardly deny you your own wine!'

'It has been an honour and a pleasure getting to know you all,' said Michaleto, pouring himself a goblet and then settling down between the Lessini twins. 'And so, to celebrate our ever-lasting friendship, I bring you treasures from the East ...'

He clicked his fingers, and his page set the chest down on a low table. 'My thanks, Corallino,' Michaleto said kindly. 'Time for bed now, eh?'

'Yes, sir,' the boy agreed gratefully, and he withdrew with the other servants.

Upon opening the chest, Michaleto took out his brass water pipe and assembled it on the table. He filled the base from a water jug and then fetched a hot coal from the fireplace to put in the head. He had first introduced his new friends to what he called a *huqqah* several nights before, and had shown them how the Arabs smoked dried hemp leaves.

'Are you sure it won't drive us all as mad as they are?' Bruto scoffed as Michaleto tested the mouthpiece.

'Well, I can't promise,' he replied with a wink, and offered him the hose.

Bruto took a long draw before emitting two plumes of

smoke from his nostrils like a surly dragon. The ladies were next to partake, Nerissa and Melania showing genteel and prudent restraint, while Arianna inhaled enough to make herself choke!

Dionigi followed, and he passed his smoke back to his cousin with a kiss that made the others cringe. Thankfully, Vitale and Ariello were quick to follow it with their own "kiss of smoke" parody, which conjured enough hilarity to quell the awkwardness. Ariello passed his smoke on to Mercutio, who intended to keep the joke going; but when he turned to his neighbour, he found himself faced with the humourless Bruto, who turned away. So, he blew it in his ear.

Once Michaleto had entertained them with a few smoke-blowing tricks, he returned to his chest and removed a small silver box. 'Now, for the real magic,' he said gleefully.

'What have you there?' asked Dionigi, drawing near.

'Magic from the forest,' Michaleto whispered, as though their voices would disturb what lay within. He lifted the lid carefully and they all gathered round.

'Michaleto, no!' Nerissa protested.

'Peace, cousin,' he replied, laughing. 'It is the last night of the *Carnevale*, after all. You would not want our guests to think you a mean hostess, would you?'

'What are they?' asked Mercutio.

'The essential ingredient to any fashionable party, this year,' Michaleto answered, picking out one of the curious little mushrooms from the box and holding it up for them to see. 'The fairies' ambrosia. The source of all their power and longevity. Now, mere mortals such as we may never hope to become what they are. But, with a taste of these, we can take a glimpse into their world ...'

His eyes settled on Mercutio, and he handed him the first mushroom.

'Are they really magic?' asked Arianna.

'Only one way to find out,' Mercutio replied, and they all watched as he popped it into his mouth and started chewing.

The silver box was then passed around and the others followed suit — all except Nerissa, who abstained discreetly — and Melania, who took only the daintiest bite.

'Nothing's happening,' Mercutio reported once he'd swallowed the last of the spongy flesh.

'Give it some time, my friend,' Michaleto reassured him. 'Your night has only just begun ...'

By the time they had made their way out of the palace and onto the street, Mercutio had begun to wonder if he was still awake or dreaming. Every light he passed — be it candle, lantern or torch — seemed to shine with its own halo of colours. Looking to the sky, he saw that the same was true of the stars: each one radiated waves of prismatic light, more breathtaking than the aurora borealis.

Immersed in this new world of euphoric sounds and colours, he watched his companions disappear into the crowd thronging the Piazzetta San Marco, trails of coloured light glowing in their wake. He turned to the waterfront and gazed out at the lagoon, a glimmering sheet of indigo in the night. Venice was disorientating, and he could not be sure if the black land he saw yonder was the mainland or some other island. Then, it occurred to him: Verona was still the place he returned to when he dreamed, so he must be awake.

Passing the lofty heights of the *campanile*, Mercutio joined the masses singing and dancing in Saint Mark's Square. He marvelled at the fabulous masks and costumes surrounding him, their textures and colours more rich than he had ever seen before. He frolicked with jugglers and flirted with fire eaters, who blew flames for him that bloomed into magical birds, circling and soaring into the night.

Beyond the square, he joined a band of jolly minstrels, marching and singing in time to their tunes. They paraded across a canal and into a public garden festooned with paper lanterns. Amid the revellers on the green, Mercutio saw the Queen of Egypt dancing with a group of French noblemen.

'My mother is of your country, *messieurs*,' she told them fluently.

'But, of course, we knew this from your excellent tongue,' they gushed, prompting the ibises on her gown to fan their wings with pride.

Mercutio blew a kiss that flew to her like a butterfly; then, he proceeded to a small square beyond the garden, where he found Sock and Buskin engrossed in the tricks of a street magician. Emerging on the Grand Canal, he came across wily Odysseus introducing Spartacus and the Crusader to a group of feisty courtesans, who Mercutio thought looked "cocky" in more ways than one. Shrieks of cruel laughter drew his attention to the icy

65

water, and he spotted Alexander boarding a gondola with his Persian queen, who stumbled into the vehicle.

Mercutio turned into a side street and found himself wandering a labyrinth of lanes and alleys, their stone walls rippling around him like silk. He reached out to touch them and recoiled when his fingers sank through their surface. Hopping to avoid a puddle of urine, he marvelled at how it simmered and bubbled on the cobbles. When he closed his eyes, his mind was flooded with patterns of a million different colours, many of which he'd never seen before and knew he'd never see again.

Opening them, he found himself standing before two large timber ramps rising to meet each other over the Grand Canal. The Rialto Bridge groaned with revellers crossing between the districts of San Marco and San Polo, but, to Mercutio, they were mere blurs of colour and sound. Halfway across, he stopped and looked out over the water …

Arms embraced him from behind. A chin settled on his shoulder. Soft curls tickled his ear. Tingles began to creep up his spine and dance across his scalp, resounding sweetly in his ears. He felt so at peace that he leaned his head back and sighed. These couldn't possibly be a stranger's arms.

'How now, *il Callipigio*?' uttered the lips close to his ear.

Mercutio turned around to behold a young man in a fox mask, his form vividly clear amid the passing blurs. The man reached out and lifted the porcelain mask from Mercutio's face — a gesture he was compelled to return.

'Romeo!' he cried, and threw his arms around him. 'How came you here?'

'It was not so difficult,' his friend replied, patting his back. '*You* managed it, after all. Despite what my good parents say, I had to see the *Carnevale*, if only once. And I had to see it with you. You've no idea how bored and lonely I've been, without you.'

'Can it really be you?' Mercutio wondered, touching Romeo's face. It was warm, it was flesh, it was real.

Romeo took him by the hands and pulled him close to kiss him. A soft, gentle kiss, at first; but there was something in his lips that invited an audacious ardour and returned it in kind, like the natural ebbing and flowing of the tide. They had kissed before — as children, in play or moments of joy and jest — but never before had it felt so sweet. It was bold and emboldening; certain and ascertaining. It was the declaration and the sealing of

67

their bond. It confirmed all the things Mercutio had ever thought and felt and wanted: to know that he was loved by the one he'd loved so long.

The world seemed a different place when their lips parted: better, brighter, warmer and full of promise.

'I want to speak,' Mercutio began, 'but I ...'

'Tonight, wit resides more in lips than in tongues,' said Romeo. 'There is more eloquence in a sugar touch of them than in all the sonnets of Italy.'

Mercutio had always felt at war with the times for loving Romeo — as though his heart were some arcane relic of bygone days, when Alexander had loved Hephaestion and Hadrian had adored Antinous — leaving him besieged on all sides by the age of his existence. 'But maybe ...' he uttered, 'maybe peace *can* be found ...'

'We'll find it,' Romeo assured him. 'Mercutio, time has taught me that, whoever else may come and go from my heart —'

'Bianca Vespeti, Silvia Acerbi, Agnese Strafatta, Virginia Montecchi, Rossana la zingara —'

'Just so! But, despite those who've come and gone, your place in it has never waned.'

'I know it. I just didn't know if you loved me the *way* I love you.'

'And now?'

Mercutio smiled. 'We feel the same. The question is, what can we do about it?'

'This, for one thing,' Romeo replied, and he teased him with several more kisses.

'Why can't it always be this way?' Mercutio wondered.

'I suppose because we're not free to do whatever we want, back home,' said Romeo. 'But here … Here, it feels like we can do anything!'

'Until we go home.'

'Who says we must go home?'

'We would stay here? For how long?'

'Who knows? As long as we live? Maybe longer?'

Another smile. 'That's all right, then. Now, let's get a drink. Then, how about a play? *Un Capitano Moro*'s supposed to be a good one!'

Together, they crossed the bridge into San Polo. The rest of the night was a whirlwind of drinking, dancing, kissing and revelling. They dodged egg-throwers and shunned fortune-tellers: for they were young; what need had they to know or fear the future? Instead, they joined the wanton masses chasing green dragons, blue fairies and white rabbits, bereft of their wits with wonder.

In time, their adventures brought them back to Saint Mark's Square, where a great crowd had gathered to watch the burning of a giant effigy of Pantalone, the grotesque antagonist of a popular morality play. As the flames grew higher, they all joined in chanting, 'It's going! It's going! The Carnival is going!'

The bells of San Francesco della Vigna began to toll, their mournful notes marking the end of the festival season and the start of Lent.

'Ash Wednesday,' said Mercutio, noting the pale dawn breaking in the eastern sky. He turned to Romeo — but Romeo wasn't there.

The crowds were dispersing, and they had been separated. Mercutio tried to reach him, but they were driven farther and

70

farther apart by the relentless surge of people. Soon, there were canals between them, and each time Mercutio looked for a bridge to cross, he lost sight of Romeo altogether and all sense of direction. A panic rose in him that he would never see Romeo again if he did not catch him now. It made him sick and dizzy, as though his head were floating away from his body. He had to close his eyes.

He woke in his bed at the Doge's Palace. His first thoughts were of the decision he and Romeo had made as they'd watched the burning of Pantalone. They would not return to Verona, but would stay in Venice together. They'd write to tell their families so and to crave their support. Perhaps they would take up life as poets or artists, feeding and clothing themselves with rhymes and brushstrokes and odes to the Doge's blessed niece! Two blissful bachelors devoted to each other.

But something was wrong. The bleary haze of sleep was clearing from his mind, unveiling a monstrous headache and a growing unease.

The door opened and his valet entered, carrying a jug of hot water and fresh linen.

'Orazio …?' Mercutio murmured.

'Yes, sir?' the man answered.

'Is Romeo here?'

'Romeo, sir? Romeo *Montecchi*?'

Mercutio knew the answer from the man's sheer bewilderment.

'No … No, I meant one of the footmen. Romeo Veniero. He owes me for a bet on a boat race.'

'Had a good night, did you?'

'Best night of my life …'

'I thought as much when those two soldiers carried you home. Said they'd found you passed out in the piazza. Luckily, they were Veronese — troops from our escort, no less — so they knew where to bring you and to ask no reward for their trouble.'

'Did you get their names?'

'Lancillotto and Galeatto something …'

'Find them. Give them my purse.'

'But there's over a hundred ducats in it!'

'Better make it up to two hundred, then!'

'Yes, sir,' Orazio yielded, though he would disregard the last instruction.

As his valet pottered about the room, Mercutio found himself coming to the awful conclusion that his meeting with Romeo had been impossible. There was just no way he could have appeared in Venice and then disappeared, all in a matter of hours. But what of the plans they'd made to stay? The notion began to unravel before his very eyes, its logic crumbling in even the weakest daylight as Orazio opened the shutters to admit the cold morning.

'What infernal bird is that?' Mercutio snapped.

'The lark, sir. The bird of morning.'

'The bird of mourning,' Mercutio said darkly.

The rain came that day as if last night's revels had moved God to break His oath never to punish mankind again by flood. The Doge had invited Verona's delegates to a special Lenten service in Saint Mark's Basilica, where they joined the congregation of Venice's elite.

As the Latin sermon got under way, Mercutio's mind stole back to the night before. Had it all been a figment of his intoxication? Or had he mistaken a stranger for his beloved friend? Had it been someone he knew? A classical god in mortal disguise? Or had it been the Devil, come to torment him? He thought of that silly, podgy little fellow from his priest's textbook: all bandy legs and wonky horns and pointing phallus. It had always made him smirk. But he remembered now that Lucifer had been beautiful before he fell. An angel as fair as he was, in fact. He had been the shining one, the bringer of light, the Morning Star heralding the dawn.

When his turn came, Mercutio knelt before the Patriarch of Venice to receive the sprinkling of ashes on his head.

'Remember, man, that thou art dust, and to dust thou shalt return.'

The Veronese began their journey home the following day, their convoy laden with chests of silk, spices, salt, and the finest Murano glassware: all gifts from the Serene Republic to the Prince of Verona.

Mercutio's last impression of Venice was of a chilling damp

that permeated every stone. Upon a stormy grey sea, beneath an iron-grey sky, everything was wet.

He told no one of his experience at the *Carnevale* — not even Benvolio, once they were reunited. Yet, he began to consider if there might have been some way that Romeo *could* have come to Venice. According to Benvolio, Romeo had been ill while Mercutio was away, having taken to his bed with influenza. Benvolio attested to having seen very little of him, and Mercutio supposed that could have been the opportunity he'd taken to leave Verona secretly and join him in Venice. It was not so impossible, after all! But he knew in his heart that it was more far-fetched than Leander swimming the Hellespont, and he could not bear to even broach the matter with Romeo himself.

Thus, Mercutio came to know true suffering as to finally obtain that which one's heart desires most, only to wake the next day to find that it is lost. Not a day passed that he did not long to return to that magical night of the *Carnevale*, and he had been haunted by dreams of Venice ever since.

VII

Is Not This Better Now Than Groaning For Love?

THE morning after the Capulets' summer ball, Mercutio woke in his bed in the little house he rented. He had been so drunk come daybreak that he did not remember the Lessini brothers carrying him home, nor Orazio putting him to bed. His first awareness was of sunlight dancing on his face; then, a stamping in his head. He tried to raise himself up, but a tidal wave of nausea knocked him back down.

'Am I at sea?' he murmured. 'Did those bloody actors sell me to pirates?'

'No, sir,' Orazio replied, pouring him a cup of water. 'Sir, your friend is waiting for you, downstairs.'

Romeo.

Mercutio made another attempt to get up, finding some success in crawling on his hands and knees; but a misplaced hand saw him tumble out of bed and hit the wooden floor.

'Don't make him wait for me,' he said as Orazio helped him to his feet. 'Give him breakfast and tell him I'll be down, anon.'

He washed hastily and combed his hair, all the while trying to maintain a basic sense of up and down. Once he'd clambered into a pair of hose, he threw on a clean shirt, kicked on some shoes, took a swig from his water cup, and then flew down the stairs, losing a shoe on the way.

Entering the small parlour, he found Benvolio perched on the windowsill, absorbed in a copy of *The Decameron* by Boccaccio. With his free hand, he was dipping sops of bread into a bowl of spiced milk and honey.

'Have you nearly got to the end?' Mercutio enquired. His friend nodded absently, so he remarked, 'It's such a shock when they all die of plague.'

Benvolio looked up sharply, the book dropping to his lap. 'You've spoiled it!'

'I jest, I jest,' Mercutio tried to say, wrestling his laughter.

'So, they *don't* die of plague? Then, you've spoiled that, too!'

'You are too hot this morning and need cooling down! What do you say we go for a splash at the baths?'

'But — I've already had a bath, this morning.'

'*So*? You can have another, to make up for the one you skipped yesterday.'

'Oh, no, Mercutio. Last time we went, you got water in my ear and I couldn't hear properly for two days, after.'

'All the better, then, to guard you against careless tongues that would spoil every book you haven't finished!'

Soon enough, the two friends were on their way to the old Roman spa near the Piazza San Zeno. Seeing as Benvolio mentioned nothing of Romeo, Mercutio decided not to either. He felt so uplifted in Benvolio's company, strolling through busy streets bathed in glorious sunshine. The despair that had swallowed him whole like a great leviathan seemed to have released him and retreated, now. But he knew he was still at risk — that the monster lurked somewhere in the depths.

Though Benvolio had complained, he was as excited as

Mercutio the moment he saw the cool water glinting amid the colonnades. They relieved themselves of their clothes in an ante-room before racing to the water to join the other bathers, Mercutio as naked as a Roman statue, Benvolio wrapped in a *perizoma* loincloth.

Once they were submerged, Mercutio stripped his friend of his undergarment, proclaiming, 'You are just as male as the rest of us, Bino. Be proud! Some fellows are far worse off!'

Before his friend could object, Mercutio was wearing the loincloth on his head. 'You cannot shock Sister Mercutia, my dear boy,' he said in a reedy voice, 'for I have seen it *all* in my time.'

Benvolio knew better than to quibble with Sister Mercutia: it was how he'd ended up with water in his ear, last time!

'Oh — did I tell you what happened, last night?' he asked.

'What of last night?' Mercutio replied, a sudden knot in his stomach.

'After you and I parted ways, I met up with Abramo and Gaspare. Baldassarre was with them still, riding on Abramo's shoulders and singing with his eyes closed. They swore they'd only let him sip the dregs of their tankards, but they knew that their master, my uncle, would not believe it. So, they were avoiding taking the boy home till he was fast asleep.'

'Oh, the corruption of youth!' Mercutio declaimed, rolling his Rs.

'We had fun, though,' Benvolio continued, giggling. 'Gaspare dared Abramo to blow on his torch, and his breath lit up the street like a dragon. There was an old beggar-woman who ran screaming for her life!'

'She were a witch, upon my life, to fear an honest fire so.'

'Call you mischievous men and alcoholic fumes *honest*?'

'I see your point. She were a saint, then, to flee such wickedness! I, on the other hand, abandoned myself to mischief, alcohol and wickedness with the Lessini twins and their troupe. We honoured the Lady of Verona with a circle dance and then crossed the Pietra Bridge to the grounds of the old Roman theatre.'

'Marry, in the dead of night? I should not have been so bold.'

'In truth, Bino, you would have swooned: for we found there a company of ghosts staging a play.'

'Never!'

'I tell you the truth. They seemed not to mind us, though, and welcomed us to their production.'

'What was it?'

'Tediously brief, and a very tragical mirth.'

'Now, I *know* you are pulling my leg.'

'Oh, was that your leg? But I jest with you only to avoid the shocking truth, which I do not think you could endure to hear.'

'What? What is it?'

'In the theatre ruins, I saw the shade of a woman, as clearly as if by daylight. She was walking along bent-double — much like your beggar-woman, I imagine — clutching her back as she went …'

'Who was she?'

'It was the Empress Messalina.'

Benvolio bit his lip against the laughter. 'It was not, Mercutio!'

'I tell you, it was,' Mercutio insisted. 'She was hobbling along and I heard her lament, "O, my back! My aching back! All

81

that time I spent on it, in life; why did I never think to use a cushion?"'

It was as gratifying as ever to see his friend lose to the laughter.

When they had finished at the baths, Mercutio and Benvolio headed into the Piazza San Zeno, where they found some familiar faces.

'Bardolfo! Ilario! How now?' Mercutio hailed them. 'What brings you here? And why have you the innkeeper's son and stable boy with you?'

'We are teaching Tobia and Peto how to enjoy their youth,' Bardolfo replied.

'Their master works them too hard,' Ilario explained, 'so, the slaves are in revolt! At least … until opening time, I hope.'

Having nothing better to do, they settled together on the cool steps of the basilica, chatting idly as they basked in the morning glow.

Mercutio had been glad Benvolio hadn't mentioned Romeo. But, the more he thought on it, the odder it seemed, as if his friend was avoiding the subject as deliberately as he was. But why should he do that? Now seemed as good a moment as any to find out, so Mercutio stretched and then remarked:

'I wonder where Romeo might be, this fine morning?'

'In truth, no one knows,' Benvolio replied. 'I have not seen him all this while. Though, I did see Baldassarre on my way to yours, and he told me that Romeo had not come home last night. His mother, my aunt, could not rest for worry, and had sent Baldassarre to ask Friar Lorenzo if he knew anything of Romeo's whereabouts. The boy was on his way when I spoke to him, else I'm sure he would have shared with me what the good Friar had to say.'

From his words, Benvolio seemed oblivious to his cousin's new attachment, and the last thing Mercutio wanted was to tell him of the girl on the balcony.

'Our friend must still be moping over the Rose that would not bloom,' he said. 'He'll be out amongst the sycamores, sighing to the wind and sobbing into the earth, bless him. That western grove's a veritable graveyard to the loves that boy has lost. A cemetery of broken hearts! He'll be there now, fashioning a new stone angel, and he shall kiss it and call it "*la bella* Rosalina".

83

And why not? It'll be just as fair and twice as warm as the real one!'

'That reminds me of what else Baldassarre said,' Benvolio exclaimed. 'Apparently, a letter arrived at the house this morning, addressed to Romeo. It had been sealed hastily, and so had opened in Baldassarre's hand. He admitted to reading it in the hope that it might shed some light on Romeo's whereabouts. What he found instead was a furious challenge from Rosalina's cousin, Tybalt!'

'Poorly written, no doubt,' Mercutio scoffed. '"If ye come sniffing round my womenfolk again, it is *you* what will get penetrated".' He turned to their friends, grabbed his crotch and cried, '*En garde!*'

'They say that Tybalt guards his kinswomen jealously,' said Benvolio, 'and that he tried to have his sisters committed to a convent! If he believes he has cause to quarrel with Romeo, then I am afraid for my cousin.'

'How is Romeo's swordsmanship? Good enough to contend with the Prince of Cats?'

'I cannot remember the last time he took instruction with our tutor. He and *maestro* Giasone are practically strangers to one another.'

'I'll wager he knows his poetry master well enough!' said Bardolfo.

'Perhaps he can disarm Tybalt with a sonnet!' added Ilario.

'Is Tybalt really to be feared?' Benvolio asked.

Mercutio sighed and scratched his head. 'Well, you know that Tybalt is nephew to Orlando Capuleti and his vain wife,' he said, 'but he is also nephew to Achille Cattanei, of the Cattanei School of Fencing. All the Capulet boys go there for training — and the girls, too, that have hair on their chests! Lo and behold, Tybalt emerged as Uncle Achille's *star* pupil. He fights as well as you sing at recitals — oh, do not blush, Bino, you know you have a lovely voice! But, when it comes to swordplay, Tybalt is the *primo uomo*. He knows it all and can do it all. Though, every man has his weakness, and his is surely his temper!'

'I know it well enough. I met him in the fray yesterday, and, when I entreated him to help me restore peace, he tried to cut my ear off! I think he is no Christian, but a disciple of Mars! I fear he will not mind the Prince's decree until it is too late.'

'What is there to fret about?' Mercutio snapped. 'Our

85

Romeo has already died a thousand times before! Pierced through the heart by as many arrows. Slain by that blind, heartless fool who flaps about on chicken's wings. Only last night, he drowned in the pools of a fair maiden's dark eyes.'

'Dark? I thought *la bella* Rosalina's eyes were light ...'

'Well ... *you* would know. You've spent more time admiring them than I have.'

Benvolio's cheeks flushed again, and Mercutio wondered if he teased his friend as much as he did purely for the charming effect it had on his face.

'You know how your cousin gets when his heart becomes set on a girl,' he said in a lighter vein. 'Compared to *her* glory, Petrarch's Laura was a scullion! Dante's Beatrice can go to Hell! Queen Dido was Queen Dowdy. Cleopatra? Ha! A common gypsy-girl. Helen a whore and Hero a harlot, not worth the trip to Troy or the swim to Sestos. "Thisbe had a blue eye or two," he'd grant you, "but I should be Mercutio's lover if I loved only for blue eyes!" He is like that Lesbian — that poetess of the Greek isle — who relished nothing so much as cracking oysters and slurping clams. Personally, shellfish has always made me queasy —'

'I thought you enjoyed a *cockle*, now and then,' Bardolfo interjected.

Mercutio was about to retort, but Benvolio laid a hand on his shoulder and quoted, '"When wrath runs rampage in thy heart, thou must hold still that unruly tongue."'

'Or engage it elsewhere,' Mercutio returned, and he attacked Benvolio's face like an ecstatic dog.

As Benvolio wiped the slobber from his cheeks, he spotted a sprightly figure approaching. 'It's him,' he cried. 'It's Romeo!'

Though the sun was in his eyes and he could not see, Mercutio felt a sudden thud within his chest.

'Speak of the Devil and his horn doth appear,' he said airily.

'That's *horns*,' Benvolio corrected.

'So it is. And here comes the horny Devil, now. Well, Lucifer, what have you to say for yourself? You led us a merry dance last night!'

'What? Are you angry with me, dear Mercutio?' Romeo replied, unable to restrain the joy lighting his eyes and filling his voice.

'*Angry*? When I got home, I checked my face in the mirror for signs of plague. For it could only be that, I said to myself, that could have caused Romeo to shun his friends as though his life depended on it!'

Romeo laughed and pulled him into a hearty embrace, kissing his lips and holding him tight. He then did the same to Benvolio, but his cousin fended him off.

'Cousin, you are still wearing last night's clothes,' he complained. 'Have you not washed and changed all this while?'

'It still *is* last night, as far as I'm concerned,' Romeo declared, 'and may it forever be so! Forgive me, both of you. I had such business as to pardon any man for neglecting his friends.'

'Certainly,' Mercutio replied. 'After all, what importance are friends when compared to the business of giving one's buttocks a good flexing?'

'Perhaps that's the secret to his shapely arse,' said Ilario, slapping Romeo on the rump.

'There's a new pearl of wisdom, if ever I heard one,' said Mercutio. 'The health of a man's love life may be discerned by the condition of his buttocks. Be they firm and buoyant: he has

88

found a regular nymph to his satyr. Be they flabby or thin as a friar's cheeks, however, and I'm afraid he's destined for the priesthood. Pray, Benvolio, write that down.'

'Is it so, *signor* Romeo?' asked Peto.

'Ask me not,' Romeo deferred, 'when you can ask *il Callipigio*, himself.'

'Ask not *il Callipigio*,' Mercutio returned, 'for he will answer you through that for which he is so admired!'

'I think we've discovered Mercutio's secret, too,' said Tobia.

'Whatever do you mean? You know full well I am a virgin!'

His company could not stop laughing for some time. And so the bantering continued, and the steps of the basilica became as merry as an alehouse.

'You see,' Mercutio said to Romeo closely. 'Is this not better than moping and mooning for love?'

Romeo smiled at him.

'What on earth's *that*?' said Benvolio suddenly.

Looking across the piazza, Mercutio instantly spotted the

89

huge woman processing towards them, a mousy-haired youth at her side. Veiled and wimpled as she was, she could have been mistaken for an abbess, if not for the voluminous layers of gaudy fabrics she had swathed herself in. The pomposity she exuded made her all the more ridiculous, and Mercutio's eyes sparkled with mischief as he jumped up and cried:

'A sail! A sail!
Nay, no ship,
but a whale!
Dost thou see her fat tail?
Why, I thought she was male!'

Climbing up Romeo's back, he mimed shielding his eyes from the sun. Then, he pointed and cried, 'Thar' she blows, lads!'

'She could yield enough oil to light the lamps of all Verona,' said Benvolio.

'Do not let her hear you,' Mercutio cautioned, 'lest she cough up her ambergris and we are all drowned!'

The woman stopped before the steps and affected a curtsey

to them.

'God ye good morrow, gracious Madam,' Mercutio spoke for them all.

The woman cleared her throat to reply; but then she turned to her attendant and snapped, 'Pietro, my fan!'

The mousy-haired lad handed her an embroidered paddle, which she swept genteelly before her face.

'What a relief,' Mercutio muttered, and his companions began hissing and shaking with suppressed laughter.

'What say you, good sir?' the woman demanded.

'Oh, merely that a fan offers fine relief from the afternoon heat,' he replied.

'After noon? It cannot be so late.'

'Why, look there, gentlewoman,' Mercutio bade her, indicating the sundial on the basilica wall. 'You will see that the naughty hand of the dial has its grip firmly on the hot prick of noon.'

The woman squawked. 'Get away! What sort of gentleman are you?'

'One, My Large Lady, whom God has made for himself to ruin.'

'Oh, yes,' the woman said knowingly. 'My brother was one of those. I shall tell you as I told him: repent, keep to a life of celibacy, and you shall be forgiven it, hereafter. Now, which one of you would be young Romeo?'

'Well, I *would* be,' Mercutio quibbled, 'if I *was* he.'

'I too, at that,' said Benvolio, sniggering.

'And I!' the others chorused.

Just as the woman took a great breath to scold them, Romeo stepped forward.

'I am the one you seek, Madam,' he said, his radiant smile an instant cure to her choler.

'Oh, er … well …' she said, blushing, 'if thee be he of the House Montecchi, then I would have a confidence with thee.'

'Does she not mean *conference*?' Benvolio whispered to Mercutio.

Even as he snickered, Mercutio felt his heart sinking. The woman had been familiar to him from the start; but now he remembered why. She had been attending Narcisa Capuleti at the ball, last night. She was the Capulets' nurse, and had come, no doubt, to communicate some secret business between Romeo and his new love. The girl on the balcony.

'No, no, Benvolio,' Mercutio burst out, 'I tell you the veil's to hide the fact the woman's a hoar!'

'What's that word, sir?' the Nurse asked sharply.

'Hoar? Why, one whose hair hath turned hoary-white with age,' Mercutio explained.

'Then, thou gives me double cheek, for I am neither so aged, nor whorey!'

'Indeed, I have a double cheek, Madam, and you may kiss it at your leisure.'

The Nurse squawked again, but she could not make her obloquy heard over the crude song Mercutio began — concerning hoary hares and hairy whores — while he flitted around her like a gadfly.

'Good Mercutio,' Romeo intervened, 'will you leave me now, to my business? I will come to you, after.'

Mercutio was arrested mid-lyric. Romeo's eyes shone in the

93

sun like blue opals, their gentle pathos reaching deep into Mercutio's chest and lifting his heart again. He was not forgotten.

'Are you going to your father's house for lunch?' he enquired. 'We'll meet you there.'

'I ... will not be there for lunch,' Romeo admitted awkwardly.

'Dinner, then! It is your turn to host Benvolio and me, since we have fed you this last fortnight.'

'Very well, then. Come, both of you, to my father's house at six, and we shall dine.'

Satisfied, Mercutio turned to Benvolio with a wink. Then, signalling to the others to follow, he led his merry band of idlers from the basilica steps and into the piazza, singing his song of hares and whores at the top of his voice.

VIII

We Waste Our Lights in Vain, Like Lights by Day

I⊤ was just before six in the evening when Mercutio and Benvolio arrived at the Palazzo Montecchi. Crowned with M-shaped merlons, its battlements declared it to the city as the seat of the Montecchi family, though the whole neighbourhood was dotted with the houses of their kin, including that of Benvolio, which was but a street away.

The two young men were admitted to the palazzo's interior courtyard, where they were quickly met by Baldassarre.

'Good evening, gentlemen,' he greeted them.

'What's this, boy?' Mercutio asked amusedly. 'Go and fetch that errant master of yours and tell him to come and greet his guests, himself.'

The servant-boy looked surprised. 'My master is not at home, sir.'

'Romeo not at home?' said Benvolio.

'Hell's teeth!' Mercutio exclaimed, stamping his foot.

'He was expecting us at six,' Benvolio explained.

'You are more than welcome to stay,' Baldassarre assured them. '*Signor* Romeo may return at any time. And there is plenty of supper that I may serve you.'

'I did not come here to dine with *you*, boy,' Mercutio snapped. 'How can we possibly dine at a man's house without the man here to host us?'

'Surely, such formalities do not apply to friendships as old as ours?' said Benvolio.

'I' faith,' Baldassarre agreed.

Looking from one benign face to the other, Mercutio huffed in submission.

Baldassarre took them to a cool parlour near Romeo's quarters, where he seated them at a table before a fading mural of the Last Supper.

'Are my good aunt and uncle at home?' Benvolio enquired as the boy laid out their plates and cutlery.

'My lord and lady mean to rise at dawn for matins,' he answered, 'and have retired early to bed.'

'Then, my parents have surely done the same,' Benvolio remarked.

Mercutio rolled his eyes and settled his head on his hand.

Talk of Romeo's parents prompted him to reflect on his own relationship with them. Federigo and Beatrice Montecchi were upstanding citizens of Verona: charitable, godly, and loving parents to their only son. They treated Mercutio with perfect civility; yet, he'd always felt that they *tolerated* his friendship with Romeo rather than approving of it. It was hardly surprising: he was, after all, notorious for his wild ways and lack of piety. Every parent worried about bad influences on their child; but Mercutio wondered sometimes if there was more to it. Had they noticed something about the way he looked at their son? Did they see the torch burning in the silence?

He ate little food and said even less, though he was not so reserved with the carafe of wine. His mind descended into the deep red liquid and stewed in thoughts of where his absent friend preferred to be. Was he at the balcony in the orchard, again? Or on the road to Mantua, his new love at his side? Perhaps they were knelt in a chapel that very moment ...

'I really am quite vexed with Romeo,' said Benvolio, chewing a leg of roasted pigeon. 'Tomorrow, we must get to the bottom of all this distraction. I had thought *la bella* Rosalina at the heart of it; but, now, I am not so sure —'

Mercutio stood abruptly.

'Forgive me,' he said, 'but I think I'll be on my way, now.'

Without another word, he marched out of the Palazzo Montecchi and into the streets, heading for his house, the blue sky above him fading in ochre light.

Arriving home, he called to his valet and began throwing off his clothes in the hallway.

'Change of plan, Orazio. I'm going to that Bonifati thing, after all. Lay out my costume for me, would you? And tell Angelino to bring me some soap and fresh water.'

'Your page has returned to his parents' house for the night, sir,' Orazio informed him. 'He'll be back first thing, tomorrow.'

'Angelino gone, too? This will be his mother's doing! Still,

98

donna Ippolita doubts my fitness to mentor her son. I suppose she wants another chance to interrogate him about me!' He sighed. 'So, I must do without my page tonight ... So be it.'

Going to the wash basin in his bedchamber, Mercutio rinsed the afternoon sweat from his body and dabbed himself with a little musk amber. Once he'd checked that his face was still smooth enough from his last shave, he began dressing. Orazio helped him into a fresh lawn shirt and a pair of particoloured hose with leather soles. The doublet he donned was one of grey and silver brocade, as dark and glinting as storm clouds.

Sitting down in front of his Venetian looking glass, Mercutio took up a small bowl and mixed a dollop of beeswax with an ounce of gold dust he'd bought from the apothecary's. He combed the glittering paste through his hair, using wavy strokes, until his locks were transfigured into solid gold. Now, he was the complete image of a classical sculpture come to life; a gilded idol consecrated to the Sun God of old.

He held a mask of filigree gold to his eyes while his valet tied the cords behind his head, careful not to smear his hair. Then, he put on a cape of saffron-dyed velvet, which Orazio fastened with a cameo brooch of the dancing Hours leading the

Horses of Helios.

Bereft of his page, Mercutio sent for Gaspare to light him to the Palazzo Bonifati.

The Bonifati were the most affluent family of Verona's growing merchant class. Their paterfamilias, *signor* Lunardo, hailed from Venice originally, born in the boat-building district of Castello. He'd had the uncommon fortune to be educated at a friary, which had led to an apprenticeship with a trading company and a career travelling the Silk Road as far afield as Somalia and China. Lunardo had dreamed of starting up his own business one day, but Venice was teeming with self-made men, all vying to build their empires on top of each other's.

Seeking pastures new, he'd explored Padua and Vicenza before settling in Verona, where he'd joined the city's Guild of Merchants. His venture had paid off, and he'd made his fortune bringing Venetian commerce to the inland state. His next endeavour had been to marry into the upper classes by wedding *donna* Patrizia, a daughter of the noble Pindemonte family. This venture had yielded three children, but failed to admit him into high society: for he would always be a tradesman and an outsider.

Still, if he could not win over Verona's elite, he would spare no expense in wooing their children. Thus, *signor* Lunardo had instructed his young son and daughters to host a lavish masquerade for the city's socialites while he and his wife were conveniently away on business.

Mercutio arrived at the Palazzo Bonifati soon after nine o'clock. Gaspare had been trying to persuade him to smuggle him in as well, but Mercutio sent him on his way with a silver ducat and a kick up the rump. Entering the palazzo gates, he followed the allure of music and firelight along a dark passageway …

Suddenly, he emerged on a courtyard lit with dozens of paper lanterns. *Signor* Lunardo's passion for exotica was no secret, but Mercutio had never imagined that walking into the man's house would be like entering a Moorish palace. All around him stood Byzantine columns and horseshoe arches, punctuated here and there with potted fig trees and damask rosebushes. Central to the courtyard was an immaculate lawn with a bubbling fountain, inlaid with turquoise and lapis lazuli. On the grass, a quartet of musicians sat on a Persian rug, welcoming the guests with jolly tunes. If Mercutio could not find distraction from his troubles here, there was none to be found!

'Welcome to the Palazzo Bonifati, *signore*,' said a young footman, whose looks made Mercutio think of Mizi Xia. 'May I offer you a cup of wine? If you turn your attention to the lawn, you will see that the fountain flows red, tonight. Guests are free to refill their cups whenever they please. May I wish you a very good night!'

Mercutio raised his cup to the man and drained it in one draught.

There was so much to see that he hardly knew where to begin. In the arcade closest to him was a collection of birdcages, some as extravagant as palaces; so he strolled over to take a look. The tropical specimens perched within were like none he'd ever seen before: speckled kingfishers and fruit-coloured canaries, their plumage as vivid as tempera paintings. While he contemplated how far these birds had travelled to be there, his ears caught the most unexpected words. Advancing to the next cage along — a grand pagoda of gilded rattan — he found a lime-green parakeet with a rosy beak.

'Say it again,' he encouraged.

'*I love you*,' the bird repeated, hopping down from its perch and waddling towards the bars. Mercutio watched, agog, as it proceeded to *cheep* and squeak a chaotic tune for him, bobbing its head up and down. '*I love you,*' it croaked once more.

'You remind me of someone I know,' Mercutio said wryly.

'*You look gorgeous*!'

'You too.'

It was a strange thing, but Mercutio was suddenly filled with sadness. The magnificence of the birds and their dwellings seemed to fade away, and he saw only their confinement, their captivity, their slowly breaking hearts. He'd buy them all just to set them free. But where would they go? How could they live?

'I see we are Brother and Sister, tonight,' said a velvety voice, just as he caught the scent of *essence de jasmin* in the air.

'*Bonsoir, la belle,*' he said with a bow. 'There's a French salutation for your fancy French ear. Now, here's an Italian one for your other …' and with that, he leaned in and kissed Melania's cheek.

'I must say, that's quite a feat of alchemy,' she said, marvelling at his gilded hair. 'It really is something to see the Sun come out at night! I only hope my efforts shall not be eclipsed.'

Mercutio stepped back to admire her. Behind her satin eye-

103

-mask, Melania's beauty shone as radiantly as the moon. Her gown was of midnight-blue velvet and white silk brocaded with silver stars, its close-fitting design lending her silhouette a sleek elegance. Her hair had been wound into a dark chignon and studded with twinkling pearls, while her smooth brow glimmered with a circlet of sapphires and silver crescents.

'Enchanting,' was Mercutio's verdict. 'How kind of you to give up the Hunt this night to carouse with us.'

'And just in time to save you from a night of making conversation with talking birds. What did he have to say?'

'How do you know it's a *he*?'

'I always know,' Melania replied. 'You missed the fireworks, by the way. There was a little display going when I got here. You'd think the Bonifati might have waited till more of their guests had arrived!'

'Speaking of which, where are our hosts?'

'Around here, somewhere, I imagine — though I've not seen one, yet.'

Mercutio coughed suddenly to alert her to someone approaching behind, and they turned together to greet that someone with gracious smiles.

'Welcome, *signorina*, *signore*,' said a nervous young man, bowing to them like a servant. 'I am Prosperino Bonifati. Forgive me for not greeting you sooner. There's been so much to organise, tonight — without my sisters, I don't know how I would've managed — oh, not that I'm complaining! It is a pleasure to host you all. My apologies, once again.'

'Think nothing of it,' Melania reassured him, patting his arm. 'Your servants have been more than attentive. I only regret that we have not had chance to spend any time with you.'

'Oh … The regret is mine, *la bella*,' Prosperino replied, reddening.

For the son of the richest merchant in Verona, Prosperino Bonifati was not at all what Mercutio had expected. He'd pictured another Dionigi Urbana, with all the traits typical of a spoilt, sinful son and heir. But Prosperino was no such thing. Mercutio could tell at a glance that he was shy and unassuming by nature, with a gentle heart not unlike Benvolio's. He was also far healthier-looking than the likes of Dionigi, whose relentless pleasure-seeking had drained his youth beyond his years. Prosperino was still unspoiled: his black curls thick and shiny, his eyes large and liquid grey, his olive skin as smooth and glowing as a child's.

'We hear your parents are in Venice,' Mercutio remarked. 'That's always the best excuse for a party!'

'Yes, indeed,' Prosperino agreed.

'We were at the *Carnevale*, this year,' said Melania. 'Have you ever been?'

'Well, once I —'

'Look, there they are,' said a loud voice. 'I knew we'd find them, somewhere!'

Across the courtyard, Dionigi had emerged from the palazzo as though he owned the place. Goblet in hand and flanked by his usual followers, he looked like a Roman boy-Emperor observing the rites of Bacchus. His costume was best described as a long silk tabard held together with gold fibulae at his shoulders and a filigree belt around his waist, which just about prevented it from opening at the sides and exposing his naked body. His grey head was crowned with a wreath of ivy leaves and berries, while his skinny arms were coiled with gold serpents and draped in a new leopard skin.

106

'Mercutio!' cried Arianna, rushing to him for hugs and kisses. She was feeling particularly overjoyed for some reason or other, and had clearly decided to make Mercutio the object of her elation. 'How divine to see you! You look … divine! Do you like my costume? I am Titania, Queen of the Fairies.'

Mercutio stepped back to look at her. She was wearing a slinky *chiton* of raspberry-red silk and sheer muslin, which revealed far more flesh than Melania deemed necessary. Glazed moths had been pinned as brooches along her neckline, while jasper cameos linked filigree chains around her waist. Her brassy hair was curled and pinned in a classical style, topped with a crown of dainty flowers. She made sure Mercutio had a good look at her new rings: moss agates etched with floral cameos, and a gold one starring a butterfly frozen in fiery amber.

'Queen of the Fairies?' he said. 'I'd have thought that was more your cousin's niche.'

'I am Oberon, the Fairy King,' Dionigi proclaimed. 'My interests include little Indian catamites and inciting my queen to fornicate with farmyard animals.'

'It's a lie!' Arianna jested.

'What have you done to poor Caligula?' Melania asked,

touching Dionigi's pelt.

'Grew too big to handle,' Dionigi replied. 'More trouble than he was worth, so I put him to a better use.' He looked her and Mercutio over. 'So, no Mercury and Venus, tonight?'

'Time for a change,' Mercutio said airily.

'I see. So, who are we, tonight? Let me guess … I have it! You are the terrible twins of Delos. Well, Phoebus Apollo I can just about accept — for Mercutio is a light around which the world revolves — but do you not think the Virgin Huntress is a bit of a stretch for you, *la bella*?'

'Think less Virgin and more *Huntress*, perhaps?' Arianna suggested.

'Oh, I see,' Dionigi said slyly, before whispering loudly, '*She always gets her man.*'

'Not as often as you,' Mercutio retorted.

'Shame you can't say the same for yourself,' Dionigi replied. 'Oh, well. Let's get on with drowning our sorrows, shall we?'

His proposal was met with rapturous cheers from his followers, and he grabbed a startled Prosperino by the waist before leading them back into the palazzo.

'Is he wearing any underwear?' Mercutio asked hotly.

Melania sniggered and shook her head. 'Are you?'

Mercutio's laughter answered for him.

He offered Melania his arm, and they strolled to the wine fountain to refill their cups. Dionigi's parting remarks had rankled him, but he tried to dismiss them. There was no way he could have been alluding to Romeo ...

IX

If Love Be Rough with You, Be Rough with Love

T HE Bonifati masquerade proved to be a world apart from the genteel, family occasion of the Capulets' summer ball, both in the conduct of the guests and their hosts' ability to manage them. The young Bonifatis were nowhere to be seen, leaving it to the servants to stand in as hosts, between chasing empty goblets rolling about the patios and striving to keep the lawn free of olive stones and fruit rinds. Prosperino remained a hostage to Dionigi and his crew, who had pressed him into giving them a complete tour of his home. Word was that his elder sister, Prudenzia, was busy trying to reach their vintners for more wine, while his younger sister, Lucrezia, had withdrawn to her boudoir after taking ill or something.

Following Dionigi's example, many guests had disappeared

into the palazzo to explore its inner reaches; but Mercutio, for one, preferred the courtyard's space and open air on so warm a summer's night. He and Melania toured the arcades, arm-in-arm, revisiting the birdcages and the rose-ringed parakeet. His feathered flatterer would not speak to him again, however, and Mercutio walked on with a strange pang of sadness. Then, he passed a couple who applauded his "solid-gold" hair, and he was filled with the pride of the Sun God once more.

They followed the paths of white-and-blue tiles around the lawn, admiring the mosaic work beneath their feet, its geometric style so unlike the portraits and landscapes they had known all their lives. Looking up, they viewed a range of Persian rugs hanging from the upper galleries, each one a work of art and available to buy, no doubt. They found vases of Ming porcelain filled with peacock plumes, as well as pots of exotic shrubs they had never seen before: showy camellia bushes, their flowers so smooth and their leaves so shiny they could have been carved of wax; oriental poppies, their petals so vibrant yet delicate as tissue paper; dwarf trees from China, arranged with rocks and mosses to create miniature landscapes.

'That one looks like … like a *place*,' Mercutio said in astonishment.

'They're called *penjing*, *signore*,' said the young footman who had greeted him earlier. 'In my homeland, the Emperor is said to have thousands of *penjing* in the gardens of his palace. One for each of his concubines.'

Mercutio laughed. 'What is your name?'

'I'm called Zuan, *signore*,' the youth replied.

'Tell me, Zuan,' said Melania, her eyes glowing like sapphires, 'does your homeland have an Empress?'

Zuan barely had time to tell her anything of the Empress or the hierarchy of consorts and mistresses beneath her — which never failed to capture the European imagination — or of the woman who had once risen from lowly concubine to rule the empire in her own right and found her own dynasty; or how empresses had tried to emulate her for generations after: for Zuan was soon called away by a drunken couple in desperate need of the privy.

'That'll be us ere too long, with any luck,' said Mercutio, and he led Melania back to the fountain for more wine. As he dipped their cups into the font, there was a commotion behind him.

Melania glanced over his shoulder and sighed. 'Here she comes, again …'

It was too late to hide. Mercutio turned around and was instantly accosted.

'Have *you* seen him?' Arianna asked.

'Who, Arianna?'

'That man, over there — look!' she said excitedly.

Scanning various clusters of people around the courtyard, Mercutio had no idea who he was meant to be looking at. However, the moment he saw a figure slip from one of the clusters and disappear behind a pillar, he knew he'd found the object of Arianna's excitement. The man was tall and dark and dressed in a dashing costume of black and red velvet, its tight fit accentuating his strong, masculine build. His face was fiendish and deathly white — which Mercutio attributed to some kind of mask — which would also account for the black-lacquered horns that curled from his forehead.

'Was that him?' Melania asked, looking too.

'The one with the horns,' Arianna replied. 'Nobody seems to know who he is.'

113

'Is that not the point of a masquerade?' Mercutio asked.

'Apparently, he hasn't spoken a word to anyone all night. I thought he might be a Spanish prince or something, but Dionigi reckons he's one of *signor* Lunardo's trading contacts from Arabia. I bet he could tell us a thing or two about Eastern "pastimes". I hear they've got illustrated manuals and everything!'

'Begging your pardon, *signorina*,' said a maid, who was passing with a tray of watermelon slices. 'I cannot tell you who that gentleman is, but he is of *no* connection to this family. What's more, three ladies have complained of his lechery, this night. I am sorry to say that includes *signor* Bonifati's youngest daughter, Lucrezia, who is but a girl of fifteen and innocent as snowdrops. The dear child had come to fetch me from the kitchens when she found the gentleman skulking in the hall. He made rude advances towards her — which she rebuffed with all the goodness of little Saint Agnes — but the heathen dared to put his hands on her!'

'How uncivil,' said Mercutio, trying to be serious, but he could not ignore the shoulders shaking either side of him, and he burst out laughing.

114

'Oh, how I wish I'd been there to see that!' Arianna cried. 'Can you imagine the look on her sweet face?'

'The little novice surely thought it was Satan,' Melania replied, 'come to carry her away to the underworld,' and they both laughed together.

The maid excused herself curtly, though not before Arianna had taken one of the melon slices from her tray.

'Perhaps we should find darling Lucrezia and ask her what she knows of our mystery man?' she proposed, tossing her watermelon to the ground after one bite.

'Was that not pleasant?' Mercutio enquired.

'It was delicious. Why?' she answered.

Having found a partner for her sport, Arianna embarked on the hunt for Lucrezia Bonifati, Melania in tow.

Mercutio had become overwhelmed with the urge to dance. It had nothing to do with the quartet's jolly tunes, however, but a bladder nearing bursting point. Dario directed him into the palazzo and down a corridor lit with torches, where he found a small room with a hole in the ground. He spent a good few minutes relieving himself of all he'd drunk that night, giggling

115

for no better reason than that he'd been surrounded by people only minutes ago, but was now standing alone in a room with his penis in his hand.

He left the privy feeling calmer and more clear-headed. Then, he remembered that clear-headedness was not the state he wished to return to tonight, and he quickened his pace back to the fountain. Turning a corner, he almost walked face-first into another man, skulking in the gloom. Mercutio snorted in annoyance; but a few steps on, he paused. *Black and red velvet*. The silence was so absolute that, as he looked back, he half expected the man to have vanished as suddenly as he'd appeared. But no: he was still there, watching him. Mercutio saw his ghastly face in detail now, and it was not a mask at all, but black and white tempera, which had been used masterfully to paint his face with a fiendish skull. His eyes were so deep a shade of brown that they glowed red in the torchlight, burning in their black sockets with the impassive certitude of a lion.

Mercutio was about to ask the man if he spoke Italian, but before his lips could part, the red eyes loomed closer. Hot fingers closed upon his wrist. Excitement fired every nerve in his body as he was pulled to a dim alcove and pressed to the wall. His instinct was to resist — to fight — but, the moment fiery lips were

116

upon his, he was transfixed. A powerful mixture of lust and exhilaration ignited in his mouth and surged to his loins, and he kissed the man back as though the thirst would kill him. He wanted to run his fingers through the stranger's hair — to pull its sleek blackness and feel its strength — but his wandering hands were seized and pinned to the wall. Perhaps now he should be afraid; but as the man resumed the passionate communion between their mouths, Mercutio found himself yielding, melting. Ecstasy overrode all else. He gasped as hungry lips found their way to his throat, and he did not catch his breath again until —

Suddenly, people flooded the hallway ahead, bringing noise and more light. The man tensed in Mercutio's arms like a startled cat. Only one of the crowd was observant enough to spot them, and she was coming towards them at a languid pace. Without a word, the skull-faced man pulled up his hose and took off in the other direction, disappearing into the darkness.

Deserted, Mercutio closed his eyes and rested against the wall, trying to calm his pounding heart with slow and even breaths.

'Well, well,' he heard Melania say as she slinked to his side. 'It looks as though our mystery man got what he came for —

one way or the other.'

'Nearly,' Mercutio replied. 'Jealous, *la bella*?'

'Who wouldn't be? But I'd never begrudge you your thrills, my sweet. Should I lend you my fan to cool your cheeks? Or would that risk fanning the flames?'

Mercutio accepted her feathered paddle and tried to cool his prickling face.

'So?' Melania pressed. 'Who was he?'

'No idea,' Mercutio lied.

'What? You mean you went into his arms without even getting his name?'

'I do not think he could speak our language.'

'Mercutio, for shame! You're becoming worse than Arianna.'

'*Her*? Never!'

'How disappointed she'll be to have missed out. I'm only sorry to have spoiled it for you, but it couldn't be helped. You see, the wine's run out — that fountain's used it all up — and Dionigi's not a happy boy. So, we were thinking of going back to his place to raid his parents' cellar, since they're away in

Rome. Coming?'

'I'll see you there.'

'Good. And don't go getting lost on the way. You wouldn't want to fall prey to another incubus, would you? Or would you?' Pecking his cheek, she paused and sniffed him. 'Mmmm,' she purred. 'Is that you or him?'

'Away with you, hussy!' Mercutio exclaimed.

Melania strode off, but her laughter lingered.

Looking back down the hall, Mercutio gazed into the darkness. 'Miaow,' he uttered faintly.

X

Speak to My Gossip Venus One Fair Word

Unsure of the way out of the Palazzo Bonifati, Mercutio found himself back in the Moorish courtyard. The musicians were still playing, though only a few guests remained, chattering by the red fountain, which bubbled feebly now, like a severed artery. Mercutio noticed many servants pottering around, and he realised with some dismay that they had already begun cleaning up. He hated the feeling of *ending* that such a sight evoked — of time lived and lost, never to be had again. It filled him with a sudden fervour that he should not remain among the moribund, and, in his haste, he nearly collided with another young man loitering at the exit.

'Out of my way, sirrah!' Mercutio snapped.

'Pardon me, *signore*,' the man replied humbly.

Mercutio stopped. Though the fellow's head hung low, his mop of black curls was as memorable as his face.

'Marry, 'tis you, good Prosperino! Good e'en again, good fellow. Why do you look so grey? It is July, but your eyes say November.'

'My eyes have always been grey, *signore*,' Prosperino replied.

'I take your word for it. Though, when first we met, they gleamed like crystal pools on the hottest night of summer. Now, they threaten to weep like winter clouds! I hope it was not my rough speech that turned your silver lining all to lead. My mother has often charged me, "Boy! There's alchemy in thy tongue!" For she had heard how I could turn promises into gold to spend beyond my allowance, and how insults and hot words from my lips would often conjure bare steel. But enough of that! I am the Sun tonight, and by my golden head and my cloak of light, it is my duty to make thee warm and bright!'

Prosperino's smile was weak. Tonight had meant to be a small triumph for the Bonifati family, but the premature demise of their party had robbed them of all glory. Lunardo had instructed his son to write to him the very next morning with news of their success, and Prosperino now faced having to disappoint his father.

'Why don't you come with me?' Mercutio proposed.

'Where are you going, *signore*?'

'The Palazzo Urbana. Dionigi and his pack will be there, of course. *La bella* Melania, too. And anyone else who quit this place in search of deeper wells to drink. What do you say?'

'Oh, no. I have things to attend to here, and I would not like to intrude ...'

'It's not an intrusion if you're invited — and I just invited you, didn't I?'

'It is very kind of you, *signore*, but all the same —'

'Look, the way I see it, you have two choices. You can stay here, help your servants clean up, catch an early night. Then, to-morrow, you can inform your father that the party fizzled out because the drink ran dry. *Or* you can tell him you caroused the rest of the night away with the heir to the Urbana banking dynasty — not to mention the Prince of Verona's favourite nephew! Which do you think will impress Pater more?'

'Well, if you're sure *signor* Dionigi will not mind …'

'A pox on him, if he does! I'm sure he won't care in the least, as soon as he's paddling in his father's finest Sherris sack. Besides, after the way he made free with your hospitality, I'd say you were entitled to rough *his* place up, a bit.'

'It was not so bad,' Prosperino said unconvincingly. 'I had better tell my sister, if I am going out. Excuse me a moment …'

Mercutio watched as his new friend went to speak to a woman in the arcade. She shared his curly black hair, though the rest of her features were concealed behind an owl mask. He could not hear the words Prosperino murmured, but he heard her reply.

'Be careful with those people, Rino. You've no idea what they're really like! Take Xerxes with you, at least, so he can get you home safely.'

'I cannot take my servant to attend me in someone else's home, Prudenzia,' Prosperino replied. 'It would be too presumptuous.'

His sister spoke some quieter words of caution to him and then kissed him goodnight. He returned to Mercutio and they quit the Palazzo Bonifati, taking the colossal Xerxes with them as torch-bearer.

Mercutio led the way through the shadowy streets towards the financial district, where the Palazzo Urbana was situated near to the Piazza delle Erbe. Years ago, when Claudio Urbana's bank had been appointed Verona's *banca centrale* and charged with managing the state's finances, the Palazzo Urbana had been his first vanity project. Built in the style of a Roman *domus*, it stood as a monument to Claudio's fabulous wealth, as well as his idolatry of the patricians of ancient Rome. Three storeys high, with roofs of shingled terracotta, the palazzo boasted an atrium, walled gardens, and its very own bathing pool.

Coming to the portico, Prosperino dismissed Xerxes while Mercutio rang the bell.

'*Ave*, Saturnino,' he addressed the man who came to answer. 'Admit us to your master.'

'The Master's in Rome,' Saturnino replied stiffly.

'Knave! I mean the son, as well you know! Now, open up, or you'll be for the lions.'

Passing him on the threshold, Mercutio couldn't resist startling the major-domo with a theatrical roar.

Beyond the gloomy vestibule, he and Prosperino entered the atrium, where a shallow pool twinkled beneath an open skylight. Marble figures loitered in the alcoves surrounding them. Mercutio did not stare at their smashed noses and graffitied limbs, as Prosperino did. Instead, he watched as the merchant's son stepped close enough to touch the savage markings etched into their stone flesh.

Studying them a moment, Prosperino made a surprising discovery:

'They're equations … Algebra.'

'Dionigi's handiwork,' said Mercutio. 'Not the only things he defaced as a child, I dare say. Perhaps these were his way of getting back at Daddy for all those maths lessons! Still, can't run a bank one day if you don't know your numbers.'

'His answers are correct …' Prosperino noted. 'Oh, except this one —'

'I shouldn't mention it, if I were you,' was Mercutio's advice.

Proceeding through double doors, they followed the sound of

chatter and music until they came to a drawing room that opened onto a peristyle garden. There, they found Dionigi and his guests lounging around an open cask of sherry, drinking and gossiping while a weary servant played the lute for them.

The silence that fell at the sight of Prosperino made it painfully obvious that the topic of discussion had been the Bonifatis and their failed attempt at a party. Fearing that Prosperino was about to turn and run home, Mercutio gave him a bracing clap on the back. *Swallow your nerves, smile, and let your new friend do the talking.*

'Good e'en and twenty, fairy people,' said Mercutio. 'The city is a Sahara, tonight! Yet, here lies an oasis.'

'You are welcome,' said Dionigi. 'Help yourselves to drink. I would not see guests of mine thirst to death.'

By the time they had sat down with their cups, the general chatter had resumed, and games of cards and dice were under way. Mercutio ushered Prosperino into the place beside Melania on a low couch. Then, he sat himself on a footstool and sipped his sherry quietly. He'd thought he might find the skull-faced man at the Palazzo Urbana, lurking somewhere among the potted ferns and grasses, tantalising Arianna still with his elusiveness, his threatening sexuality. Mercutio, however, was not so easily bedazzled, and he wondered why she'd found it so hard to see who the man really was. *Spanish prince*, *indeed*!

Dionigi and Arianna were amusing themselves with a game of *tarocchi* cards. Leading with the King of Cups, he gloated as she picked a card from the pack and turned it over.

'Ha! The Fool trumps the King of Cups,' she crowed. 'I win!'

Scowling, Dionigi took a swig from his goblet.

'Cousin, never have I seen you so unhappy to swallow a mouthful of sack!'

'Is this to be the capstone of our evening?' he retorted. 'Children's games? The night is still young and ripe enough to exploit. Yet, here we sit, as though she were old and grey and promised to a nunnery! I didn't get dressed up to spend the night at home.'

'You are the only one here with that problem,' Arianna replied.

Dionigi jumped to his feet and rounded on his lute-playing

servant.

'Publio, you play as poorly tonight as every other night of your life,' he chided. 'Be quiet! Silence has a sweeter voice than thy lute.'

'You could do with a breath of Arabian smoke to lighten your heart,' Arianna remarked. 'A pity we fed the last of your stash to Uncle Claudio's horse. I bet it danced all the way to Rome!'

A bulk of hashish had been one of the many goods Dionigi had brought back from Venice; but his stock had barely lasted him two months. He knew of only one other place in Verona where it could be had, and his cousin's idle words had called the place to mind.

'Shall we go to la Squarcia Lenzuola?' he asked with a sudden, soft mischief.

Arianna's eyes widened with delight.

"The Torn Bedsheet" was the name by which one of Verona's leading pleasure houses was commonly known. Once a regular visitor, Dionigi had not been back since an incident with candle wax had caused a small fire. In a rare show of authority, his father had forbidden him to return, as well as curtailing his allowance. However, now that his parents were away, Dionigi was free to go where he pleased, and could help himself to the family coffers.

'Attention, everyone,' he announced. 'Those of you who are game for an adventure, fetch your cloaks. Those who aren't may go home to their beds. O, Saturnino! Bring me the keys to my father's study …'

Dionigi led his party across the Nuovo Bridge and into the district of Veronetta. Strolling along the riverfront, they came to a tall, dark building like any other, except for its timber portico, which glimmered with a hanging basin of fire, from which comers and goers could light their torches throughout the night. A collection of torch-bearers were chatting beneath the eaves, waiting to escort their masters home.

Filing past them, Dionigi thumped on the door and then spoke to the man that came to the spy hatch. His companions waited excitedly, laughing and whispering — all except Prosperino, who'd not said a word since choosing to go with them.

129

'You know me, villain,' Dionigi snapped. 'Now, fetch your mistress, and don't keep me waiting!'

Within a minute, the door opened and a woman appeared in the vestibule. Though of mature years, she was still handsome, and shaped as generously as a fertility goddess. Her curly hair ought to have been grey, but had been made red and bright with costly henna. Her clothes, too, were rich in colour, and as fine as a lady's.

'*Signora* Dora! Enchantress!' Dionigi gushed. 'Too long has it been since I beheld your fair and kindly countenance.'

'Don't give me that, you little shit!' the woman snarled. 'You're barred, remember? Now, fuck off!'

'Barred? Your best and favourite patron? How can that be?'

'Do you know how much your little antics with candle wax cost me in repairs? Not to mention they nearly cost us all our bloody lives! Oh, I know I'm for the Flames in the next life — but I don't intend to let them have me in this one!'

'Come, now, *signora*. It was only a little fire. Do say we can be friends. Speak me but a few fair words and I shall make you amends.'

'*My mother's cunt*. Fair enough for you?'

'I'm afraid I've never met the lady to judge.'

'Well, that makes two of us.'

Dionigi sighed. 'If words alone will not appease you, perhaps *this* will?'

He reached into his leopard skin and produced a fat leather purse, which he handed to her.

Dora untied the strings and looked inside. Her dark eyes reflected a sickly yellow gleam.

'Have I not said that you are always welcome at la Squarcia Lenzuola?' she gushed.

'Does she speak to the man or the gold?' Mercutio whispered to Prosperino.

'Such a sum might even stretch to the cost of a private suite for the night,' Dionigi went on, 'with wine and music and the usual … amusements.'

'I dare say it might,' Dora replied.

'Then, why are we still standing out here?'

XI

O Flesh, Flesh, How Art Thou Fishified

B EYOND the vestibule curtains, *signora* Dora took Dionigi's party into a small lobby, where a plump old man sat behind a desk, tallying sums on an abacus and jotting them into a ledger. Dora slipped the purse to him and proceeded to the stairs, where she led the way up several flights and then along a corridor of closed doors.

The walls writhed with the kind of lurid frescoes designed to fire up a man's blood and thus impel him to spend.

'That figure must be Circe,' Mercutio pointed out to Prosperino, 'and those must be Odysseus's men, whom she transfigured into wild beasts. I did not know one could ride a lion in such a fashion!'

'Here's Leda and her swan,' Melania observed.

'And those two have to be Europa and Pasiphaë,' Mercutio declared, 'taking their bulls by the horns!'

'This way, please,' said Dora, opening the door at the end of the hall.

Inside, they found two girls lighting oil lamps around a luxurious room dotted with couches, low tables and Persian rugs piled with silk cushions. Gauzy summer drapes quivered before open windows, while arrangements of myrtle and wild roses lent their beauty and fragrance to the ambient sensuality.

'Please, make yourselves comfortable,' Dora bade them as the girls came to take their cloaks. 'I shall send more attendants to you, anon. That reminds me,' she said to Dionigi, 'I'm afraid your Galateo will be unavailable, tonight. He has a prior booking.'

Dionigi fished about in his leopard skin before handing her some more ducats. 'Fetch him,' he ordered.

Dora withdrew, and a group of young men and women came to the suite shortly after, bringing with them trays of wine and fruit and musical instruments. They were by no means ordinary servants, though: they were beautiful and charming and clothed in diaphanous tunics and chemises, which did little to obscure their alluring bodies.

'Ah, now the fun begins,' said Dionigi, who seemed to know them all by name. 'Azzurra, Elacatas, you see that everyone is well wined. Rossa, you have the sweetest voice; come and sing for us. A ballad, I think. Diomo and Ciana will accompany you. Abdero, you and Viola are the best dancers; show my friends what you can do!'

Just then, the door opened and a tall youth entered, dressed in a sheer tunic over a linen loincloth. Not only was he as handsome as a Cypriot shepherd boy, but his body had the fantastic dimensions and milky smoothness of a statue, as though old Pygmalion had undertaken a second labour of love. Much of him had been painted with Venetian ceruse to emphasise his flawlessness, though his face, hands and feet remained tantalisingly bare, and his nipples glinted gold.

'Galateo, my love,' Dionigi cried. 'Come and sit with me!'

They kissed hungrily before falling onto a couch together.

Rossa was singing a prologue in her pretty soprano pitch, while Diomo blew his panpipes and Ciana fingered notes from her lyre. Arianna clapped wildly as Abdero and Viola enfolded each other in their arms and began the dance of Troilus and Cressida.

Mercutio became so absorbed in the spectacle of graceful limbs that it took him a while to realise that his nose was twitching. Over the scent of flowers and incense, he detected a strange yet familiar odour: pungent, almost sweaty, like mouldering grass, yet sickly sweet. He looked to Melania with the question on his lips, and she answered him with a glance towards Dionigi, who was puffing on a wooden smoking pipe that Galateo held for him.

'Good as the stuff we had in Venice?' Arianna asked as she came to sit beside him.

'Good enough,' Dionigi replied, exhaling a long plume of smoke.

Once Arianna had filled her lungs, Elacatas took the pipe to pass around the others.

'I have seen my father deal in such items from North Africa,' Prosperino told Mercutio. 'He keeps one in his study, though I have never seen how to use it ...'

135

'Watch me,' said Mercutio, and, acting slowly for Prosperino's benefit, he put the pipe to his lips and took a deep breath of the narcotic smoke. 'Try to hold the breath as long as you can,' he advised. 'If it's anything like last time, we're going to need food, lest we start eating each other!'

Azzurra went round with a platter of fruit, and Mercutio took a ripe peach for himself. It proved to be the juiciest, most fragrant peach he'd ever tasted, its sweetness filling his nostrils and gushing into his mouth. Its pale skin was softer than velvet stained with the rosy blushes of an angel; so much like a human cheek that Mercutio stroked it and kissed it dearly and held it to his own.

'Love of the bitten peach never dies,' he murmured.

'What does that mean, *signore*?' Prosperino asked hazily.

'Mercutio, my dear,' said Melania, leaning over and touching his shoulder, as if to wake him from a dream. 'Do not let the smoke go to your head. Here, put that peach down and have some grapes with me ...'

Mercutio did as she said. He munched on the vine of grapes she gave him, and they giggled together like children.

136

The dance of Troilus and Cressida was coming to an end —
war and infidelity having parted the lovers forever — and everyone was applauding.

'Bravo!' cried Dionigi, jumping to his feet to congratulate
the dancers. 'Now, what shall we have, next?'

'The Rape of Lucretia! The Rape of Lucretia!' Arianna
chanted.

'Forgive me, *signore*,' Viola panted, 'but I do not think I can
dance again, so soon.'

'Oh, very well,' said Dionigi. 'Azzurra can take your place.'

'No,' Arianna said proudly, '*I* shall play Lucretia. Well, I've
seen it enough times to know the role off by heart! Abdero will
help me, won't you? You always make a delectable Sextus Tarquin.'

What followed was a rather farcical rendition of the tragic
Roman legend. Arianna assumed the position of the sleeping Lucretia, reclining on a bed of cushions, while Rossa intoned the
prologue. Soon, Abdero came stalking onto the scene, his ges-
tures large and athletic as he mimed spying the virtuous matron,
admiring her serene beauty, and then vowing to Jove that he

137

would have her body. At that moment, Arianna looked up, winked at her audience, and then fell back to sleeping. Thus, the tone continued, with Arianna stopping now and then to speak to the audience and even taking their direction. By the time it was over and she took her bow, she was so exhilarated that she leapt into Abdero's arms and kissed him.

'And the moral of that story is,' she said as she returned to Dionigi and fell down beside him, 'women should not try to be too perfect.'

'You've never been in any danger there, Cousin,' Dionigi replied.

'Well, think about it. If Lucretia had been out, whoring around with the other Roman wives, she would not have fallen into Tarquin's clutches. More to the point, he would not have *wanted* her if she had proven to be unchaste. So, you see, her virtue was her undoing.'

'If that is true, then I am glad of my sins,' Melania said drily.

'I'm sure you're not the only one, *la bella*,' Mercutio teased.

'Let Elacatas sing for us, next,' said Dionigi. 'What shall we have? Ode to Hero and Leander?'

'How about the lay of Pyramus and Thisbe?' Arianna suggested.

'No one got laid, thanks to that bloody lion,' Mercutio quipped. 'Oh, enough of Love's martyrs! I'm afraid their misfortune will be catching! May we not have some lighter entertainment? A spot of dildo juggling, perhaps? Or is there a fellow here who will light his farts for us with a candle?'

'I've never seen *that* before,' Arianna said excitedly. 'Cousin, do you think —'

'No candles!' Dionigi snapped. 'Unless *you* want to pay that red-haired witch for the next accident?'

'Let's have the ballad of Venus and Adonis,' Melania said decisively.

'Now, *there's* a lay worth hearing,' said Mercutio. 'Just leave out the grisly bit at the end with the boar.'

Diomo swapped his panpipes for a lute and began the prelude. Mercutio was fussing to have his wine cup refilled when he was suddenly transfixed, pierced by a voice so high and pure and full of power that he could have believed a seraph had fallen to earth. But it was the attendant, Elacatas, who revealed himself to

139

be an enchanting countertenor. He sang of sunlit woods and wild game and shady bowers, where a rosy-cheeked youth made love to a red-lipped goddess.

Dionigi held out his cup for Galateo to refill. Then, he removed the glass phial that he wore on a thong around his neck. Inside was the last of a dark tincture — which he'd sworn to his parents was saint's blood — and he emptied it into his cup and swilled it around. Arianna watched intently as he sipped the bitter draught, his eyes aglow. He insisted on holding the cup for her and watched, in turn, as she drank, giggling and grimacing at the taste. As she wiped her mouth with the back of her hand, Dionigi gave the cup to Viola, who was waiting to take it around.

When it came to Melania, Mercutio watched her take the cup and raise it to her lips. He was the only one to understand what happened next. Melania inhaled its aroma deeply — an action that disguised the fact that she did not actually drink.

Crafty, Mercutio thought, *but wise*. He could only imagine what the Saint's Blood tincture contained. Henbane? Datura? Tears of the poppy? Root of the mandrake? Fortified with some aphrodisiac, no doubt. Only the utterly reckless would imbibe such a thing!

The thought made him hesitate as the cup entered his hands. What harm, what dreadful price would this dark libation demand in return for a brief release from all sadness and pain? Melania was not willing to pay it. Dionigi was in arrears and growing ever more indebted to it. Arianna didn't even trouble herself to think on it; if her cousin saw no harm, neither did she. Then, there were the others — Mercutio did not know all their names — who had followed Dionigi home, then to this place, and would follow him now, into the aether.

Prosperino stirred softly beside him. He would be next to drink. Arabian smoke was one thing, but nightshades and opiates were far more dangerous. Who knew how far the merchant's son would go to keep up with his new friends?

Finally, there was Romeo. He was in that room too, lodged in Mercutio's heart. Yet, he had never felt farther away. The anger and longing still smouldered in Mercutio's chest — no longer scalding and explosive, as it had been before the gallon of wine — but a dull, tormenting burn, so persistent it made him want to cry. Suddenly, the potion in his hand seemed the only thing left in the world that might take it away. Perhaps the price would not be *too* high. Surely, one drink would not destroy him. It was not hemlock, after all.

It was settled in a second. Putting the cold pewter to his lips, he drained the cup of all its magic and poison, his ears ringing with the beauty of Elacatas's voice:

> *'Since thou art dead, lo! here I prophesy,*
> *Sorrow on love hereafter shall attend:*
> *It shall be waited on with jealousy,*
> *Find sweet beginning but unsavoury end;*
> *Ne'er settled equally, but high or low,*
> *That all love's pleasure shall not match its woe.'*

The taste was bitter beyond belief. Mercutio wiped his mouth on his sleeve and then passed the vessel on to Prosperino, not looking to see how bemused, annoyed or relieved he was to find it empty. He stuffed a handful of grapes into his mouth to banish the taste and then reclined, closing his eyes. Each breath he took became slower and deeper, and he fancied he could hear the very beats of his heart, easing to a gentle pulse.

What were those words Elacatas had sung? A curse. Venus's curse! Adonis had been slain by the wild boar, and, as the goddess wept over his tender body, she vowed that, henceforth, Love would bring more suffering to the world than it ever would peace or joy.

Mercutio opened his eyes. Finally, it made sense. Love was a torment to him; but it was to Romeo, too, whose heart had been broken a hundred times. Even Benvolio suffered in his way, loving those who forever overlooked him for his modest and mild nature. And it was all because Venus had cursed Love, aeons ago!

Mercutio thought of the Piazza Erbe and the archer in the sky, and of his fits of mania that only Romeo could allay. Now, he knew why:

'*Love shall be raging mad, and silly mild,*' he quoted the goddess, '*Make the young old, the old become a child.*'

It seemed to him that all the woes of the human race could be traced back to this ancient malediction. He had not realised he knew the words by heart, but they surged to his lips and he joined in the song:

> '*Love shall suspect where is no cause of fear;*
>   *It shall not fear where it should most mistrust;*
> *It shall be merciful and too severe,*
> *And most deceiving when it seems most just …*

143

It shall be cause of war and dire events,
And set dissension 'twixt the son and sire;
Subject and servile to all discontents,
As dry combustious matter is to fire:
Sith in his prime Death doth my love destroy,
They that love best their loves shall not enjoy.'

XII

With Him, Patroclus, Upon a Lazy Bed

'Are you well, *signor* Mercutio?' asked a gentle voice that could have been Benvolio's, but more likely belonged to Prosperino. Mercutio could not answer in any case, for he was affected by the sudden immensity of the room. The walls must still be there, *somewhere*, he supposed; but, as far as he could see, there was only velvet darkness and the lights of candles, floating around him like stars in the night.

There was another sensation, as though time itself was expanding, as if years were passing with every moment. Yet, Mercutio was unaltered. He was not ageing or changing in any way. His hands remained as smooth and strong as ever. The fabric of his clothes were not fraying or fading. *This must be immortality*!

145

Finally, it had happened: he'd become a divine and ageless being, like those he masqueraded as so often.

Looking around, he saw that he was not alone. His fellow immortals were all about him. There was Bacchus, the young yet ashen-haired god of wine and revelry, teasing the Princess Ariadne, his consort-cum-high priestess. She had bared her breasts to show off her gilded nipples, and Bacchus decided to bless them with the contents of his wine cup. He poured his next cup over the erotic sculpture of Galateo, reclining beside him, so that he might have the pleasure of lapping it from the well of his navel.

A murmur drew Mercutio's attention to the lost boy, Ganymede, slumped at the other end of the couch. His grey eyes were red and hazy, and he was fighting to keep them open. In the struggle, he ran his fingers through his black curls and began pulling at them.

'How did I get here?' he asked fearfully. 'How do I get back?'

'Peace, peace,' Mercutio said softly, taking his hands and settling them in his lap. 'Sleep, now. You'll feel better when you wake.'

The youth laid his head back and allowed his eyes to close. Mercutio smoothed the curls from his forehead and left him to sleep.

Moving on, he spotted a dark goddess lounging among silk cushions, whom he first took for Diana the Huntress. A retinue of young nymphs attended on her, fetching her wine and dates and figs and honey. A mirror was brought and held up before her, so that she could watch as they combed her luxuriant hair. Mercutio realised, then, that she was not Diana at all, but Venus incarnate. She inspected her reflection with a majestic nonchalance, but he knew that cunning belied the poise. With the looking glass now in her hand, she could watch all around her with feline subtlety.

Mercutio wished to be out of her sight. He was sure she'd seen him stroke Ganymede's curls, and it troubled him to think what she might make of it. So, he wandered the infinite cosmos of the room, searching for the door. Somewhere beyond the Milky Way, he could hear Pan, the woodland god, playing his pipes with his Roman brother, Faunus. Then came the ribald tones of Sylvanus, regaling the pretty Pleiades with tales of lush pastures and lonely shepherdesses. In a corner of the galaxy, Vulcan sweated and grunted with Virgo, close to an eruption,

147

while the over-endowed Priapus ran about the universe with his hose around his ankles, promising nymphs and satyrs alike that he could go all night.

At last, Mercutio found a door handle, though it seemed to be hanging in thin air. Nevertheless, when he turned and pulled it towards him, a tall rectangle opened in the darkness. Stepping through, he found himself back in the corridor of closed doors and lurid frescoes, which now appeared to go on forever without end. Declining to panic, he reminded himself that such things hardly mattered, now that he was a god. Only mortals ran out of time. He need simply follow the images he remembered and he would surely find his way out.

'Pasiphaë … Europa …' he noted aloud, 'Leda and her swan … Circe and her sailors …'

'What do you mean "not loud enough"?' came a strident voice.

Ahead, Mercutio saw *signora* Dora talking to a middle-aged man in one of the doorways.

'Screaming? You didn't say you wanted screaming, *signore*,' she continued. 'Screaming costs extra, you see, on account of the disturbance to my other guests.'

The half-dressed man fumbled about in his purse and then handed her some coins.

'All right, Verde,' Dora called into the room, 'give the gentleman earache, will you!'

Closing the door on them, she was about to walk away when the young man with gilded hair caught her eye.

'Well, now,' she said, 'you're one of *signor* Urbana's party, aren't you? Finished already, have you?'

Mercutio laughed. 'I'm afraid your enchanted island has failed to make a beast of me.'

'Oh, we can't have that! Love's a difficult spell to cast, it's true, but who on earth would do without it?'

'The wise, perhaps? They say Minerva was chaste, do they not?'

'She did not dwell *on earth*,' Dora pointed out. 'Besides, you don't want to pay her any mind. She never had any fun!'

'Surely, you, of all people, know that Love is a cursed thing? A chalice poisoned by Venus herself. And do you know what the cruellest part of her curse was? She made Love mortal and gave it a life span shorter than our own, always dying before we do.

149

Thus, she condemned us to know what it is to fall out of love, and, worst of all, to lose the love of those we still adore ...'

'Are you a philosopher, *signore*?' Dora asked, her voice soft as a whisper. 'Never mind. Here, it is no matter who or what you are: only what we can do for you. I hope you'll pardon me if I say that I think I understand you, *signore*, and where your "interests" may lie. Seeing as you look the sort of fellow who can well afford to indulge his interests, why don't you come along with me to the rotunda?'

Before Mercutio could muster a reply, *signora* Dora was leading the way along the hall and he was following. It was the strangest thing, but they seemed to be moving with an uncanny slowness, as if wading through a dream. He was sure that, if he were to fall over at that moment, he would be slower than a feather to hit the ground. The most curious specks of light trailed in Dora's wake, glittering like fireflies. Mercutio rubbed his eyes in disbelief, but they only shone brighter.

Turning the corner, they came upon two naked women in Roman helmets, prodding at each other with wooden swords as a flabby old man cheered them on.

'Take it back into your room, Monsignor,' Dora warned

him, 'or there'll be trouble, again!'

As the man and women left the hall sheepishly, Dora brought Mercutio to a door behind a red curtain. On the other side, they entered a private room, perfectly round and lit with hanging oil lamps. The walls were draped with golden gauze, and a smoking censer sweetened the air. At the centre of the round room was a round bed, its sheets of stainless silk.

'Welcome to the rotunda,' said Dora. 'Shan't keep you waiting a moment ...'

She disappeared, and Mercutio sat down on the bed. Leaning back onto his elbows, he drifted into a blissful lethargy. As his eyelids drooped, he had the vaguest memory of something he was supposed to be upset about. But he couldn't quite recall what it was, any more. Nor did he much care. It was far easier to just let it go.

A clap of hands brought him back to consciousness, and he sat bolt upright. *Signora* Dora was standing before him, and a procession of barefoot youths was filing into the room. They formed a circle around the bed, and Mercutio looked to Dora.

'Right, *signor* Apollo,' she said to him, 'where would you like to start?'

He did not immediately understand her, but hopped to his feet.

'How about this one?' Dora suggested, indicating the young man closest to her. 'He is named Giacinto, after the mortal youth who made love with the sun god, Apollo. An ideal match for you, I'd have thought.'

Mercutio looked at Giacinto. He was a year or so younger than him, and wonderful to behold. His hair was a mass of fiery-red curls, which hung around his chiselled face, where brown eyes glowed amber in the lamplight. His smooth, sun-kissed body was draped in a brief *chiton*, flaunting his sculpted shape.

'No?' Dora ventured. 'Well, I dare say redheads aren't for everyone.'

'I like red hair,' said Mercutio.

'Why, thank you,' she replied, patting her own. 'I like to think it's money well spent. Would you believe I was as blonde as you are, when I was a girl? No? Neither would I. But Crisippo was, and still is, as you can see ...'

Mercutio followed her direction to the next youth in the circle, who was surely as beautiful as an angel. Crisippo was even fairer than Mercutio, Dora explained, for he had come originally from the lands beyond the Rhine. His wispy hair glimmered silvery-white in the lamplight, though even more striking was the powder-blue light of his eyes. His creamy skin glowed with a rosy bloom, which filled his cheeks and lips and coloured his willowy limbs. The *chlamys* cloak draping his shoulders and the linen cloth wrapping his loins both lent him a princely air.

What was it Dora had called him? Crisippo? Of course! Chrysippus, the beautiful Prince of Elis.

Mercutio remembered the story from his boyhood, when Franciscan friars had attempted to teach him Greek and Latin. Chrysippus was the favourite son of King Pelops, and was so handsome and athletic that Laius, the king of Thebes, fell madly in love with him. While escorting him to the Olympic Games, Laius abducted Chrysippus and seduced him. It had all ended in tragedy; but Mercutio recalled conflicting accounts. Friar Teodosio's text had described the seduction as a rape, and that Chrysippus had slain himself in shame, thereafter. It was for committing this most bestial of sins, the Friar explained, that Laius, his kingdom, and his son, Oedipus, were all destroyed.

153

However, Mercutio recalled another text by a Greek mythographer mistaken for Plutarch. It told of how King Pelops had forgiven Laius for running away with his son once Laius and Chrysippus had convinced him their love was true. Pelops had welcomed them back to his court, but his queen was infuriated. She knew that Chrysippus, though illegitimate, was so favoured that he would likely supplant her own sons as heir to the throne. So, she hatched a plot to murder him and incriminate his lover. One night, she stole into the bedchamber that Laius and Chrysippus shared. Finding them sound asleep, she drew the Theban king's sword and plunged it into her stepson. Laius was arrested for the crime, but Chrysippus saved him by naming the true culprit with his dying breath.

There were several other versions of the death of Chrysippus, but it was the one by Pseudo-Plutarch that had stayed with Mercutio all these years.

'*Signore*? *Signore*?' he heard Dora say, and he realised she'd been talking to him. 'I was just saying that you're more than welcome to choose Crisippo, but there are one or two others you might like to see, first.'

'Show me.'

154

'These two, we call Hylas and Iolaus,' she said as they approached a pair of young boys, enfolded in each other's arms. 'Originally from Syracuse. Their names honour the two youths of legend who were both princes, Argonauts, and the lovers of Hercules.'

The boys were a perfect mirror to each other, Mercutio observed, from their sweet faces framed with shiny black curls, to their pretty hazel eyes and ruddy-brown complexions. They had been dressed in matching *exomis* tunics and headbands of braided gold, all of which Mercutio found utterly charming; but they were still children in his eyes, younger even than Baldassarre.

Dora was shrewd enough to see this and wasted no time in moving him on.

'Ahh,' she said with glowing confidence. 'May I present Patroclo? Imported from Constantinople. Greek stock, naturally.'

Mercutio had seen him before she'd spoken: a young man around twenty years old, standing next in the circle. Of course, he was handsome, but what made him so outstanding was the heroic quality of his features and the dignity of his bearing. In fact, Mercutio was sure he'd known his name before Dora had ever spoken it, for he could have been that very same Patroclus of Homer's *Iliad*, having stepped from the pages of the epic poem to grace the physical world. His hair was the way Mercutio had always imagined a Myrmidon warrior's: sandy brown and growing to his shoulders, a braid or two tucked behind his ears. Mercutio was tall, but Patroclo was taller still, his sinewy form clothed in a black and blue *chiton*. His skin was as bronzed as if he'd sailed the Aegean, while his eyes reflected the sea-green depths of those same waters. There was strength and courage in them, but Mercutio also saw something of loss: a glimmering pathos that resonated with his own heart.

On Dora's signal, Patroclo undid his belt and slipped off his *chiton*. The sight of his Olympian nakedness was ravishing, and Mercutio embraced him as though he were the love of his life.

'Can you love me?' he asked in a whisper.

'I can,' Patroclo answered.

There it was, a glaring chink of reality, piercing the veil of fantasy that had descended over Mercutio since drinking the Saint's Blood. Not "I do" or "I will", but simply "I can". It had been said sincerely enough — and from lips as soft and ruddy as rose petals — but the words were conditional.

'Course he can!' Dora chimed in. 'Handsome, young gentleman like you? That's a pleasure, not a chore. Isn't that right, Patroclo?'

Patroclo nodded dutifully, but his eyes said that he would never know love again until he was returned to the arms of Achilles.

They were all lost souls, these youths, so like their classical counterparts, who had once been idolised and worshipped by the civilisation that created them. Their shrines had been places of pilgrimage, where male lovers from across the Hellenic world had gone to pledge their hearts to each other. Yet, today, they were abandoned and forgotten, their love denounced as pagan bestiality or sanitised as "brotherly", if not expurgated altogether. So, where had the likes of Patroclus and Chrysippus ended up? The back rooms of swanky brothels, catering for "special" clients with classical educations.

The strength and warmth of Patroclo's body was so comforting that Mercutio held him close a moment longer. Then, even as his own body begged him not to, he let go and was gone.

'You won't find love here, *signore*,' Dora called after him. 'Not in this bloody place! Still, we've got the next best thing.

Come on, Patroclo! Let's go and see if we can peddle you to *signor* Urbana.'

XIII

Here's Much to Do with Hate, but More with Love

BENVOLIO rose brightly at the seventh hour of the morning. Knowing that he was an early riser, the servants had already brought his breakfast to him, which he found laid out on the small table in his bedchamber. He washed and dressed first, and then sat down to eat, pausing only to pick a violet petal from his porridge.

Just as he was finishing his milk, there was a rap on the door. It opened before he could answer, and a man padded into the room.

'Good morning, young master,' he said. 'Sorry to disturb you, but I thought I'd better come to you rather than your parents …'

'That's all right, Clemenzio. What is it?'

'It's a bit awkward to explain, sir. Would you mind coming with me?'

Benvolio got up and followed Clemenzio out of his bed-chamber and down the stairs. He was led through the kitchen and into the dark alley that ran between the Palazzo Benvenuto and a neighbouring priory. Benvolio shuddered in the gloom. Just as he was considering the fact that the sun never found its way down there, no matter the time of day, he realised he was wrong. Up ahead, there was a chink of light on the wall — though that was nowhere near as surprising as the young man slumped in it. Though his head was buried between his legs, Benvolio was fairly certain he knew the fellow from his mop of golden hair, still glinting with traces of pomade.

Crouching down, he spoke to him gently:

'Pardon me, My Lord Apollo, but the sun seems to have risen without you, this morn.'

Asking Clemenzio to assist him, he began the process of un-ravelling Mercutio's limbs and helping him to his feet. Mercutio giggled and murmured as though he were dreaming as they walked him back to the palazzo kitchen and sat him down at the workbench. Once he was settled — having fallen back to sleep, face-down on the bench — Benvolio said:

'My thanks, Clemenzio. I can take care of him, now.'

'Fetch me if you need anything, sir,' Clemenzio advised, before returning to his duties.

Benvolio went to the pantry and returned with a platter of bread, cheese and grapes in one hand and a tankard of fresh milk in the other. As he set them out in front of his friend, he was startled by Mercutio's voice:

'Why am I in your kitchen?'

'Forgive me,' Benvolio replied with a chuckle, 'but I did not have it in me to carry you upstairs. Besides, I do not think my father would appreciate seeing you thus.'

Mercutio had to think for a moment; then, he remembered that Benedict Montecchi, though always kind and gracious, was a pious man and a staunch teetotaller.

'Where's that new page of yours?' he enquired, buttering himself a piece of bread.

'Still sleeping,' Benvolio admitted. 'Yours?'

'Out, sketching, probably. What a pair of taskmasters we are! Rest assured, if there's valour to be found in sleeping or sketching, they'll find it, all right!'

Just then, the side door opened rather clumsily, bumping against the wall, and a girl came in with a basket of herbs on her arm. It took her a moment to realise that she was not alone; however, the second she spotted the two gentlemen sat at the workbench, she froze. All she could think to do was curtsey to them, so she did so hastily before hurrying with her basket to the refuge of the pantry.

She had not expected to see *signor* Benvolio this morning! He might have even smiled at her. Oh, how she wished she could remember clearly! But she had been distracted by the way that his friend — the blond one with the big mouth — had looked at her with such quizzical interest. Suddenly, it occurred to her what must have caught his attention: she had woven her hair into fancy braids that morning, winding them around her head and dressing them with fresh daisies and violets. As ever, she had done so in the hope that Benvolio would see. But now his friend had seen, too! Still, she could not hide in the pantry all day; she had bread to prove and joints of rabbit to season. After a quick fumble to pluck as many of the flowers from her hair as she

162

could, she went back into the kitchen and set about her work as discreetly as possible.

She could hear *signor* Benvolio speaking softly, but, in the time that passed, she heard nothing from the other one. His silence made her uneasy, and a half-glance convinced her that he was watching her. She nearly wet herself when he finally spoke:

'You, there. Pina, isn't it?'

'Pia, sir,' she corrected, coming to stand before him.

Ah, yes, Mercutio thought, *this is the girl*. Seeing her had reminded him, quite by chance, of an old rumour that the Palazzo Benvenuto harboured a young kitchen maid who was enamoured of her master's sweet son. There had been amusing tales of flowers on his breakfast tray, as well as a painful attempt at a love poem found on the back of an old shopping list.

'*Signor* Benvolio is growing into a fine figure of a man,' Mercutio remarked, 'is he not?'

'It is not my place to say, sir,' Pia replied, turning red.

'Oh? Is that why you've not yet confessed to him how much you *adore* him?'

'Mercutio!' Benvolio reproached.

163

'No need to be modest. Modesty in one may have its charms, but in two, it becomes downright exasperating! Believe me, Pia, my dear, you'll get nowhere with these Montecchi fellows unless you spell it out to them. And, if I were you, I'd do it sooner rather than later. I mean, if you're going to spend the rest of your life working in a kitchen, you'll likely end up fat and toothless. One appetite shall be gorged if the other is starved! Now, I'm not saying that Benvolio could ever *marry* you, but he might at least make love to you enough times on this wretched workbench to quench that desperate burning for him. Then, you can both get on with your lives, sated and with no regrets. After all, a bit of fornication never hurt no one! In fact, why don't I take my leave now, so that you two can get down to it?'

'Pia, would you leave us, please?' Benvolio said hotly.

Mercutio did not look as the girl ran from the room, but he felt his friend looming over him.

'Don't strike me, Bino,' he said feebly and pointed to his head: 'I have a headache.'

'The day I strike you will be the day I strike myself for doing so,' Benvolio assured him. 'Though, how you can ask for mercy when you are so merciless, yourself, I do not know.'

164

'Well, I don't know what she's so afraid of! We're all flesh and blood, aren't we?'

'Sometimes, I wonder.'

'Perhaps she does not appreciate having her lofty fantasies brought down to the sordid ground. But her desires are perfectly natural. You're not totally without your charms, you know.'

'Well, thank you! But did it ever occur to you that I might not have feelings for her?'

'You would let that stop you from making love to the poor girl? Not very selfless, Bino. You should think of it as an act of charity. Some people give alms to the poor — you give your body to kitchen maids.'

'I do not! Now, please, let there be no more talk of ... *bodies*. I have told you before, I am saving myself for the night of my wedding.'

There were a thousand and one jokes to be made at the expense of virgin bridegrooms, but Benvolio's words were so sincere that Mercutio could not mock them. He knew his own heart and was simply holding true to it. And why should he not? Though Mercutio forever teased him for it, he had grown to love what he saw as his friend's innate goodness. At times, it was difficult not to envy him. After all, what did Benvolio ever have to fear? What did he have to regret or weep for?

'If only virtue came as naturally to the rest of us,' he said with a cynical sigh. 'You really are the best person I've ever known.'

'Again, my friend, I thank you,' Benvolio replied drily. 'I wish you were this complimentary when you were sober!'

'I think it will take a *week* to dry out, after last night.'

'Just what exactly did you get up to?'

For one startling moment, Mercutio could not remember — not a single detail — as though he had opened the book of his memory on a blank page.

'We were at Romeo's together, weren't we?' he asked uncertainly.

'Yes, but then you left,' Benvolio reminded him. 'I went home to my bed. But I can see from your splendid costume that you did not.'

'I think you might have noticed if I'd gone home to your bed, Bino!'

Mercutio told him of the masquerade at the Palazzo Bonifati, glowing with excitement as he recounted the wonders he'd seen. He also mentioned the family's pleasant young son, Prosperino; though, in truth, Mercutio no longer remembered him clearly. Hadn't he been red-haired? Or was he thinking of Michaleto Bevilacqua?

He chose to omit his encounter with the skull-faced stranger, skipping straight to the wine shortage and the revellers' migration to the Palazzo Urbana. Benvolio was always fascinated by descriptions of the Roman-style *domus* in which the Urbanas lived, though he'd always shied away from Dionigi's invitations to see it for himself. Mercutio assured him it had all been perfectly tame — no wild orgies or gladiatorial bloodbaths — at least, not until they'd moved on to la Squarcia Lenzuola.

'You went to a *brothel*?' Benvolio asked in astonishment.

'A pleasure house, if you please, sirrah,' Mercutio quibbled. 'It wasn't at all how you'd imagine. It wasn't all clenched teeth and soles to the ceiling. It was rather sophisticated, actually — as brothels go! You should have seen the big-titted bawd who ran the place. She had hair redder than a cardinal's *biretta*! She was like Circe or Calypso or something: a demigoddess presiding over an island of pleasure, where a lifetime may pass in an hour — and a fortune is spent in a minute! And all her nymphs and satyrs were no mere playthings: they were skilled musicians and singers and dancers, and they performed all night for our delectation.'

'It sounds incredible,' said Benvolio. 'Are you sure you're not pulling my leg, again?'

'The question is, are *you* sure I'm not pulling your leg? Honestly, Bino, I can hardly believe it all, myself. You don't suppose I imagined the whole thing, do you? Perhaps, if we went down to Veronetta right now, we'd find nothing but a run-down *bordello* with straw mattresses and congealed puddles of God-knows-what all over the floors!'

'Good grief,' Benvolio groaned, wanting to laugh and bury his head in his hands at the same time. To top it off, Mercutio had taken a swig of milk from his tankard and spilt it down his chin.

'I shall just have to ask Melania, when I see her next. She drinks and smokes so little that she should surely remember.'

'It would surprise me if that was not her very design: to watch and remember the indiscretions of others, as the Empress

168

Livia was said to do.'

'Have you been reading Tacitus, again? Benvolio, you know that always puts you in a bad mood! Why such rancour for the Changer of Hearts? Don't think I did not hear you scorn her the other night, too. What can she have done to offend you?'

His friend would not answer, nor meet his eye, but his cheeks had coloured with displeasure.

'I think you're still in high dudgeon over the Saint Valentine's Day ball,' Mercutio said, understanding at last. 'That was five months ago, Bino! I'd have thought you'd forgiven her, by now.'

'She's a devious vixen,' Benvolio replied sullenly.

'Oh, she worked you up all night with those sweet whispers of hers,' Mercutio recalled, 'until you wanted her so badly, you looked as though you were in danger of rupturing your codpiece! But, by the end of the ball, she'd disappeared with Francesco Gonzaga, leaving you with nothing but a bad case of blue balls. You should have asked me — I'd have lent you a hand.'

'Mercutio!'

'Well, what are friends for? Reminds me of that time I

found you in tears because you'd seen Romeo kissing your beloved cousin, Virginia. Now, there was a girl who struggled to live up to her name!'

'That was years ago. We were only lambs.'

'Well, it mattered at the time. I hated seeing you upset. Do you remember? I asked you what I could do to make you stop crying. You said, "*I don't know*". So, I told you to close your eyes, think of your precious Virginia, and then I kissed you until your tears stopped. It worked like magic.'

'I don't think I remember.'

'No? What about those games you and Romeo and I used to play, together? Despite what our priests say, there comes a time in every boy's life when we discover there is no feeling in the world better than playing with ourselves — except, perhaps, playing with each other. Oh, how simpler those days were, when all the fire and anguish of puberty could be relieved with a happy little game of Slippery Soldiers or Soapy Monkey.'

'Must we dwell on that?' Benvolio snapped, his cheeks aglow. 'It didn't mean anything, Mercutio. We were just boys, fooling around. Curiosity got the better of us, that is all. I see nothing to be proud of — except, perhaps, that we would have been defilers had we done those things with girls. But we are boys no longer, Mercutio. We are *men*, now. I would never think of my fellow man in that way, whereas you cannot seem to help yourself! At best, it is immature. At worst … it is perverse.'

'How dare you sit in judgement of me?' Mercutio bristled, and he spat his mouthful of bread back onto his plate. 'To hell with whose roof we are under! I will not swallow your vinegar and gall, sirrah! You are speaking to the nephew of your sovereign Prince, lest you forget, or have you always longed to be flogged in a public square?'

'Mercutio, I didn't mean —'

'Shall I tell you what the good people of our city say of you, *Saint* Benvolio? The same hateful tongues that condemn me as "perverse" ridicule the gentle and virtuous Benvolio as not having what it takes to make love to a woman. That his goodness and innocence render him as impotent as a child! Make no mistake, you are just as queer a fellow as I am, in their eyes. "Benvolio's blood's not so much red as lily-white. Do you suppose there's something wrong with him?" Tell me, are they right to say those things of you? Or are they being as cruel and ignorant as you have been to me?'

171

'I am sorry, my friend,' was all Benvolio could say. 'I did not mean to hurt you. It's just that I … I do not always understand you.'

'Little Benvolio, forever afraid to say how he truly feels,' Mercutio scorned. Suddenly, he was in Benvolio's face, nose to nose, blue eyes blazing into brown. 'Why not just be honest, for once? Deep down, you hate me, don't you? You think I'm wicked. Perhaps you think I'd be better off dead. Tell me, do you hope to see me burn in Hell?'

'Mercutio! How can you say such things?' said Benvolio, his eyes filling with angry tears.

'Oh, spare me your tears! What are you, a little girl?'

His mouth stopped abruptly, as though the words stung his own lips. He could see where this torrent of rage wanted to take him, how it urged him to flay and crucify his friend and suck the blood from him to feed his own ego, to heal his wounded pride.

'I'm sorry!' he blurted. 'I'm so sorry. Forgive me. These voices! They make us hate ourselves and then each other, and then we say the cruellest things.'

'What voices, Mercutio?' Benvolio asked, embracing him

172

and patting his back.

'I don't know. I don't know whose voices they are or where they come from. All I know is that they are not ours.'

'I hate no part of you, I swear. I would not change a single hair on your head.'

'Not one hair?'

'Not one. For alteration, no matter how minute, would be an alteration too much, and Mercutio would no longer be himself. He would be Tommo, Dicco or Harrio, but not Mercutio.'

'You … love Mercutio?'

'As Damon loved Pythias. I would stake my life as surety for yours. Stop smirking — I'm serious! Mercutio, I'm worried for you. You do not seem … well.'

'I am just tired. Fatigue makes monsters of us all!'

'Perhaps it is not so wise to keep company with the likes of Dionigi Urbana and Melania di Villafranca. They are hardly a wholesome influence.'

I need Romeo, but he isn't here, Mercutio nearly exclaimed. 'How do you know I'm not the bad influence on them?' he said instead.

'Was it your idea to go to a bro— pleasure house?'

'No, but I rather wish it had been. And I'm distressed to see you so positive that it wasn't. What makes you so sure?'

'Because I *know* you, Mercutio. Stop pretending that I do not.'

'If you know me so well, tell me: what am I thinking of, now?'

'Romeo.'

The frankness and accuracy of Benvolio's answer hit Mercutio as keenly as an arrow. He could feel the tears building in his eyes, against his will.

'You know, he would be worried to see you this way, too,' Benvolio continued. 'He would despair to think that he had hurt you. Romeo knows the suffering of the heart better than any of us. But there are things that have been done, now, which cannot be undone. We can only accept them and try to live with them. And may God help Verona.'

Mercutio did not ask him to elaborate. He imagined he understood well enough. A promise made in a moonlit orchard. A union between the deadliest enemies. A chalice that would poison them all.

'What must one do to earn such fearless love?' he wondered.

'Romeo loves me well enough,' Benvolio replied. 'But the love and friendship the two of you share transcends all others. I do not see that changing, come what may. Only death could come between you …'

His words had meant to be heartening, but Benvolio winced at the bittersweet taste in his mouth.

Mercutio, too, wished that death had not been spoken of so flippantly. But he also realised that Benvolio had underestimated himself earlier. He *did* understand him — at least, as far as how much Romeo meant to him.

'Good Benvolio, will you kiss me ere we part?' he asked.

'Of course,' his friend replied, and he did so, kindly. 'Must you go, now? If it is sleep you need, you can always use my bed. Then, we can go out when you rise.'

'If I do not go home soon, my valet will probably report me missing to the Watch — and my mother!'

'Dine with us here, tonight, then. I know my mother would

be glad to see you.'

'Very well. Please, tell *madonna* Irene I would be honoured.'

'Good. Try to get here before the seventh hour. And please make sure you're sober.'

'Yes, Your Highness. Anything else?'

'Yes, you are forbidden from ever speaking to Pia, again!'

'Yes, Highness! I'll not speak another word to the girl as long as I live.'

Mercutio was pulled into another embrace before they parted. Then, he left the Palazzo Benvenuto, never to return.

On the way home, he thought of Damon and Pythias. Jonathan and David. Achilles and Patroclus. Just good friends, now.

XIV

Under Love's Heavy Burden Do I Sink

ERCUTIO felt as though he could do with a good piss as he strode up the dusty street that led to his house. Ordinarily, he might have just whipped it out and gone in the nearest gutter, but the beautiful morning had brought the citizens of Verona out in full. It would be the finest day the city would see for months to come; but Mercutio took no notice. He was going home to his bed, and once he had shut out the daylight and lost himself in linen sheets, he would not rise again till eventide.

And then what? Romeo would still be absent, no doubt — ensconced in the arms of his new love, as though he'd died and gone to heaven — sparing no thought for those he'd left to mourn him on earth.

As he came to his front door, he found that it was not bolted. Thinking of the cook who leaves the kitchen door open for the errant tomcat, he slipped into the hall. However, he managed no more than three paces before he was intercepted.

'There you are, sir!' Orazio said with patent relief. But Mercutio would not encourage his fussing with kind words:

'A pot to piss in, if you please,' he requested, waiting where he stood for the man to do his bidding.

'Will you be needing breakfast, sir?' Orazio asked when he'd returned with a clean chamber pot.

'I have already swallowed more than I can stomach at the Palazzo Benvenuto,' Mercutio answered.

'Is that where you've been, sir?'

'Where else?' Mercutio asked hotly, for he was realising that there was something his servant wasn't saying.

Sure enough, Orazio produced a letter from his pocket. The sheepish manner in which he proffered it told Mercutio all he needed to know, and he did not deign to accept it until he had relieved himself at length in the chamber pot. He exchanged the warm pot for the letter — deriving a certain satisfaction from the

178

parallel — then he broke the seal and unfolded the page. His eyes fell upon solemn ink and he sighed.

> *My dear son,*
>
> *I hope all is well with you. I, myself, have not been well this week, and have withdrawn to our villa in Valpolicella. I should very much like you to visit me today, as I have one or two matters to discuss with you. I shall expect you for luncheon at midday.*
>
> *Your loving mother,*
>
> *Marzia*

If there was anything on earth that made his blood boil more than servants spying and snitching on him, Mercutio was yet to discover it.

'*Orazio*,' he said, bristling, 'it may surprise you to learn that I am going to need a bath and some fresh clothes.'

'Any particular ones in mind, sir?'

'I'm not sure, Orazio. Which do you think my *mother* would prefer?'

'I ... I really couldn't say.'

'No? You *do* surprise me. I thought that you and she might share some sort of psychic link! I cannot imagine why she feels the need to speak to me so urgently. Perhaps you know?'

Orazio did not answer, and Mercutio held him in blistering silence, watching him squirm.

'Do you remember the blue set I got for my birthday?' he asked curtly.

'Yes, sir.'

'Go and put those ones out for me.'

'Yes, sir.'

Orazio hastened off.

Mercutio was about to vent his frustrations with a terrible scream when he heard the front door open behind him. A young boy entered the hall, a bag on his shoulder and a sketchbook under his arm.

'Angelino! Good morrow,' Mercutio greeted him. 'Back from your parents' house, I see.'

'Yes, *signor* Mercutio,' his page replied humbly. 'I am sorry to have left without asking your permission, first.'

'I, too, know the howl of the dam well enough to know that it may not easily be ignored. I must answer my own mother's howl this very morning, in fact. How would you like to ride with me? I could do with a companion for the journey, and we may show Verona how far you've come in horsemanship.'

'Yes, sir,' the boy replied eagerly.

'Hurry to the mews, then, and ready our horses. Ask Gaspare to give you a hand. Bring them here and then change into your best livery!'

Angelino had dropped his bag and sketchbook and bolted out of the door before Mercutio had finished; but he was satisfied he'd been heard.

Upstairs, he found a warm bath waiting for him in his bedchamber. Orazio had also laid out the clothes he'd stipulated, and was now busying himself elsewhere. Feeling utterly squalid, Mercutio peeled off his Phoebus Apollo costume and climbed into the tub. Reclining in the warm tranquillity, he closed his eyes and sighed. The water was so soothing that he let himself slip deeper into it. Soon, it was rippling through his hair and closing over his face. Sound and light faded, and he was floating in a perfect and absolute peace ...

He heard a low, resonant *boom*. Then another. And another. Then a burst of jubilant crackles. Opening his eyes, he saw the lights of Venice shimmering on the surface above him. Fireworks soared and glittered across the night sky like Danaë's shower of gold. The bells of Saint Mark's *campanile* rang in celebration.

A young man was sitting at the water's edge, gazing down. His face was painted with the same fiendish skull as the stranger at the Palazzo Bonifati. However, the opal-blue eyes shining in his black sockets were no stranger's. Indeed, Mercutio knew those eyes better than his own. He could not be sure if the youth had seen him floating in the depths, or if he was admiring his own reflection, but he smiled fondly and leaned in to kiss the water's surface. It was only then, as the need to reach those lips overwhelmed him, that Mercutio realised he could not breathe.

Sir! Sir! a faraway voice was crying. But it hardly seemed to

182

matter. The lights of Venice were fading, and he would never reach that kiss, and it was turning ever so cold.

The next thing he knew, he was being dragged from his bathtub by Orazio. Bathwater spluttered from his mouth and nose and stung his eyes. His valet cradled him in one arm and delivered several firm blows to his back. Mercutio coughed heavily; then, he lay quite still in his servant's arms, shivering. Orazio sniffled quietly, and it seemed the most sorrowful sound he'd ever heard.

'It's all right, Orazio,' he said gently. 'I must have dozed off, that's all.'

There was something in the man's silence that told him he was not entirely believed, and he was about to give further assurances when he heard the front door again.

'Don't start much ado about nothing,' Mercutio warned him. 'You'll upset Angelino.'

Though his head pounded with all the rhythm and gusto of Saint Mark's *campanile*, Mercutio rose, and Orazio assisted in drying and dressing him. The clothes he'd chosen had been paid for by his uncle, the Prince, as an eighteenth birthday present: just the regalia he needed for a parley with his mother. The doublet was of the finest peacock-blue silk and so handsomely embroidered as to befit a prince. The hose were of pure white twill — a stately alternative to the frivolous fashion of particolouring — complete with an enviable codpiece of tanned leather. Mercutio fastened a golden garter below his knee while Orazio brought him the finishing touch: a cap of blue velvet trimmed with white peacock feathers.

When, at last, he went downstairs to hunt for his suede riding gear, he found Angelino waiting for him, gloves and boots at the ready. As Mercutio presented his hands and then his feet for his page to attire, he noted with approval that the boy was now wearing a rust-coloured tunic brocaded with gold and his best pair of yellow stockings.

'Right!' Mercutio said finally. 'Ready to ride, *signorino*?'

Processing through the Old Town, Mercutio and his page made a splendid sight upon their white stallions, the embroidery of their clothes shining in the sun like veins of quicksilver. Many people about the streets and markets stopped to watch them pass, and those indoors came to their windows and balconies to wave to them.

Soon, they reached the gatehouse of the great city wall, its turrets and battlements glowing red in the sun. They rode through the archway and into the bustling district of San Zeno, following the River Adige as it wound its way north. Watching the water, Angelino spotted a fortified tower of red brick rising from the riverbed.

'The Tower of the Chain,' Mercutio pronounced, and he explained that a garrison of soldiers was always stationed at the tower, and that they raised a great chain across the river every night to bar the way, 'Lest the Blue Serpent of Milan tries to gobble up our city while we sleep!'

Beyond Greater Verona, they found themselves in the open countryside. Mercutio had not left the city, nor even *thought* of the country, since his trip to Venice in February, when all had been grey and brown and dismal to behold. Yet, now, in the midst of high summer, the land was a radiant canvas of light and colours, more glorious to contemplate than any work of art. A patchwork of arable fields stretched for miles on either side of the river, beyond which rolled dark, wooded hills. Mercutio loved the awe with which his young companion took it all in, from the simple bank of grass beside them, dotted with vetch and lupin, to the distant spectres of the Prealps, capped in Austri-

185

an snow.

'Wishing you had your sketchbook?' he asked.

Angelino nodded avidly.

'Do you think you could sketch while riding a horse?'

'Hmm ...' the boy pondered seriously. 'I'd give it a try.'

Mercutio laughed.

It was often hard to believe that Angelino was a son of House Lupatotini, which had been a prominent military family for generations. They had produced some of the most feared and revered knights and soldiers in the province. Angelino had been named after his great grandfather, Marcangelo of San Giovanni Lupatoto, who had been a mighty warlord and a ruthless tyrant. In his lifetime, Marcangelo had murdered his own brother with poison, as well as having his first wife beheaded on false charges of adultery. He'd also feuded constantly with the Pope, and had demonstrated his contempt for the Holy Father by arresting his godson, who was serving as papal legate, and sodomising him in the town square, for which he was excommunicated.

Angelino's father, Adolfo Lupatotini, was a seasoned *condottiero* in command of his own army, who had been contracted

186

to protect Verona from rival city-states, as well as foreign invaders. Adolfo's wife, *donna* Ippolita, had hounded Prince Escalo for years to make her son page to a nobleman of his Court. Considering that Verona's security depended on her family, the Prince was loath to refuse; but it came as a surprise to all when he appointed the boy to his wayward nephew, Mercutio. Angelino's parents could hardly object, however, as it was a considerable honour for their son to be placed with one of the Prince's blood relations, no matter his suitability.

The greater surprise came when Mercutio actually rose to the challenge. He took little Angelo into his house and arranged for his tuition in every subject necessary for a boy to advance to knighthood. Yet, despite all expectations that Angelino would follow in his forefathers' footsteps, Mercutio could see plainly that the boy's passion was for art. He spent almost every free moment drawing with his charcoal sticks, and, what was more, his ability was astounding. Mercutio had seen some of his sketches lying about the house — a door, a cat, a tree, a city — all rendered with such a keen understanding of their nature and mechanics that he could not believe, at first, that they had come from the hand of an eight-year-old child.

Perhaps his family will learn to accept his true calling, one

187

day, Mercutio thought, *so long as he turns it to designing castles and siege weapons and new modes of armour*!

When the two travellers came to a ford in the river, they stopped to let their horses drink before crossing. There was something potently familiar about the spot, Mercutio thought. Looking along the bank, he spied a small, sandy beach, white as sugar, gleaming beside the water.

It had been a scorching summer's day, years ago, when he, Romeo and Benvolio were boys no older than Angelino. They had often come to the river on such days to escape the heat of the city, and were whiling their afternoon away on that very beach when a caravan of gypsies appeared on the opposite bank. The three boys watched keenly as the gypsies stopped to cool off in the river and water their horses.

Before long, Romeo jumped up and swam over to join them.

Mercutio had been puzzled, at first. Then he saw his friend talking to a girl among the travellers. She was a few years older than him, and delightfully pretty. She had the darkest skin and the longest hair Mercutio had ever seen, which swung like a rope of black silk as she twirled to the tune of her brothers' fiddles.

When Romeo finally returned, it was as if he were in a daze, though Mercutio pretended not to notice.

'Who was that?' little, doe-eyed Benvolio had asked.

'Salome or Jezebel, I'll wager,' Mercutio had quipped.

'Rossana,' Romeo had answered dreamily. 'Sana …'

He'd been in a world of his own, the rest of that day. But Mercutio had seen how happy he was, and he couldn't help but be glad for him.

He felt no gladness, this time.

XV

Summer's Lease Hath All Too Short a Date

MERGING from a leafy wood, Mercutio looked down on open hills. The land was arranged into neat and regular fields, each square assigned to the growing of apples, olives, lemons and grape vines. Every tree and crop was tended by the tenants of the nearby hamlet: peasant farmers and labourers who rented their land and homes from Mercutio's family. There was a smartness and an orderliness to the landscape here that never failed to call to mind the smart orderliness of his mother's household. Squinting against the midday glare, he pointed to a dusty road lined with poplar trees.

Angelino followed the road with his eyes to a pair of heavy wooden gates set in a white wall, which formed a perfect square around the Villa Marchesino estate. Guardhouses marked its four corners, though they had not been manned in over a hundred years and were more handy for keeping pigeons and stabling horses, nowadays. Shielding his eyes, Angelino could just about see the villa itself, its square, castellated tower rising above younger roofs of terracotta. The remnant of a Romanesque keep, he suspected. He wanted to sketch it all, there and then. And the hills. And the hamlet. And the workers in the fields.

'Did Romeo ever come here?'

'What?' Mercutio snapped. 'What did you say, boy?'

'Pardon me, sir,' Angelino said timidly, 'but I asked if the Romans had ever settled around here …'

'Oh … Yes, that is what I thought you said. Roman settlements, eh? Well, I can't promise you Capua — but stick with me, lad, and I'll find you a relic or two!'

Along the road, Mercutio saw young men in the fields, stripped to the waist, their sinews glistening in the heat, chests and shoulders heaving after a morning's toil. For a moment, he was transported to a round room, where naked young men stood in a circle; the handsomest youths that ever lived. He must put his mind to it, later, and work out where that room was exactly and how to get back to it.

Returning to the present, he noticed that he and his page had caught the attention of two old men, who were weeding among the grape vines with lethal-looking hoes. Mercutio brought his horse to a stop and touched his cap to them.

'Look at those two,' he remarked. 'Simple peasants doing an honest day's work. A gentleman should always show his appreciation to such hard-working folk. Angelino, doff your cap to them.'

'*Signor* Mercutio, I have no cap to doff.'

'So, you haven't. Hmm … I know! Why don't you flick your hair at them, instead? I'm sure they'd like that.'

The boy followed his advice and tossed his head several times, trying to flick his auburn curls as salutatorily as possible. However, it was not received well:

'What the devil is he doing?' muttered the first peasant.

'Hey, this isn't a fashion parade, you know!' cried the second. 'Why don't you save it for the Christmas pageant?'

The two men turned back to their weeding, crowing with laughter, and Mercutio instantly thought of Gaspare. This was his country, he remembered. He hailed from that very hamlet, in fact, where impudence clearly ran in the blood!

Mercutio found the timber gates open in anticipation of his arrival. *Like the doors of a cage*, he thought, and he was sure his horse shuddered beneath him as it carried him through.

Inside the compound, he looked around. The fountain in the forecourt was new, but the villa itself appeared much the same. The old tower was not as high as he remembered; though, of course, he had grown much since last he'd stood in its shadow. He still carried the boyhood image of it in his mind, its *biretta* of terracotta shingles wreathed in the clouds. Was there any chance it might have shrunk?

'*Signor* Mercutio …' Angelino whispered, alerting him to the man approaching.

'Relic number one,' Mercutio whispered back. 'God ye good morning, Glauco!'

'God ye good *afternoon*, young master,' the major-domo replied.

'A good afternoon to you, *signore*,' said Angelino. Then, he realised the conflict: 'And a good morning to you, *signor* Mercutio! A good time of day to you, both … whatever time of day that might be.'

Glauco took the reins of their horses, and, when both riders were on the ground, he offered them water. Mercutio rinsed the dust from his mouth and spat it out. Not at Glauco's feet, exactly … well …

'See that Paride gets some oats and water, would you?' he instructed. 'And do you think you could find my page something to eat and a little job to occupy him, while I'm engaged?'

'He can share my lunch in the kitchens,' Glauco replied gruffly. 'He can help me in the orchards, after.'

'Fine. Angelo, go with this man. Bring me something sweet and juicy from your labours!'

With that, Mercutio strolled on to the villa, pulling off his riding gloves with his teeth. He pranced up the steps to the portico and then entered through coffered doors. In the entrance hall, he went to the alcove and rinsed his sweaty hands in a basin of rose water.

He'd always hated coming here as a child, in the summer months, when the city heat was so stifling that paupers were found dead in the gutters, and gentlefolk dead in their beds. His mother would practically uproot their urban household to the country for a few months, complete with his elder brother and a select number of servants. Any poet would have told him what a privilege it was to spend time in a rural idyll all of his own; but, to Mercutio, it had felt more like going into exile! He'd craved the hurly-burly and the company of people, and he'd missed Romeo and Benvolio terribly. He was a city fellow, through and through, and, in his fourteenth year, he'd been such trouble during his stay that he had not been required to go back, since. Until today.

He was drying his hands on the cloth provided when he heard a shuffling on the stairs behind him. Turning around, he saw his mother's elderly maidservant carrying down a pile of linen. *Relic number two*. Even as a child, he had always despised Anselma, as she was not just his mother's confidante, but her spy. What Anselma heard, *donna* Marzia heard. What Anselma saw, *donna* Marzia saw.

Never able to resist the urge, Mercutio exclaimed:

'Anselma, you leathery old cow! Have they not sold you to slaughter, yet? Live on much longer and there'll be talk of witchcraft. Is that really how you wish to spend your last hours on earth: stripped naked and scourged through the streets to the place where they burn you?'

The woman ignored his provocations, as usual, saying simply, 'Our lady awaits you in the withdrawing room, young master.'

'Does she, indeed? Perhaps we'd better inform the Vatican!'

If anyone had asked Mercutio why he loathed this inoffensive old woman so much, he couldn't have told them. The answer had been lost to history, like the Great Library of Alexandria. But, if he had searched the recesses of his mind, sifting through the ashes of papyrus scrolls, he would have found that it was because Anselma had been the first person in his life to make him feel shame.

As boys, there had been a time when he and Romeo were inseparable. They ate together, played together, slept together. In summer, Romeo had stayed overnight at the Palazzo Marchesino in central Verona. It was that time of year when the nights were as warm as the days, and they had stripped off their nightclothes before bedding down together. There was nothing unusual about it — hundreds of boys across the Northern Hemisphere were surely doing the very same — and Mercutio had had a blissful night's sleep.

It was not until Anselma entered his bedchamber the next morning, bringing some shirts that she and his mother had stitched for him, that he had cause to worry. It was the look on her face when she saw them together: as if she had walked in on him humping Romeo's leg like a mongrel! Romeo, too, had reacted suddenly and with obvious guilt: as though he could see what she saw, through her clouded eyes.

Once Romeo had gone home, Mercutio had received a little talk from his mother. Romeo Montecchi was a nice enough boy, she had said, from a perfectly decent family, and she was sure they would be lifelong friends. But they were getting a little too old, now, to be sharing a bed — or bathing together — things of that sort. It wasn't quite seemly, any more.

Mercutio could not take her meaning, so she had elaborated:

'Romeo and you need to make sure that you do not take your friendship *too* far. Particularly in the heat of puberty. Of course, God would forgive you, but it is better to avoid the sin in the first place than to beg His pardon, after.'

Still, Mercutio could not imagine what she meant; so, no more was said about it. But he knew who was to blame. Before

197

Anselma, he and Romeo had lived together in their own little Eden. Then she had crept in, like a sneaking snake, and with her had come knowledge and talk of sin and a shame that had polluted their pure world.

XVI

Hardness Ever of Hardiness Is Mother

NSELMA opened the door for him, and Mercutio entered the withdrawing room. Considering the heat of the day, he was surprised to find it so cool. The fireplace had not been lit, of course, and the casement windows had been opened to the herb garden, its scents wafting in with birdsong on the faintest draft. Mercutio recalled the murals of courtly hunting scenes that adorned the walls of this room; but they were mostly covered with Biblical tapestries now, hanging heavily, unmoved by the breeze.

At the hearth stood *donna* Marzia, viewing some image on the wall, her hands rested upon her breast. A heavily built and imposing woman, she was dressed in a high-collared gown of voluminous black damask, embellished with white lace and

199

pearls. Anselma had tucked her greying hair into a velvet cap, which she wore with a long veil. She had heard Mercutio enter, and glanced at the hourglass on the mantel before turning to him. With a flit of her dark eyes, she appraised his courtly attire and overall smartness. Evidently pleased, she smiled faintly and reached for him, her pale fingers glinting with jewels, and Mercutio practically genuflected to kiss her hand.

'Good day, Mother.'

'Good day, my son. How was your journey?'

'Unexpected. This is the last place I'd have thought to find you, nowadays. I always had the impression that you loathed the countryside.'

'I do. Make no mistake, I would not be here if life in the city had not become so intolerable.'

'Truly? How so?'

'Where to begin?' Marzia said, sighing. 'The heat. The noise. The crowds. The miasma! I tell you, it got to the point where I could smell smoke wherever I went: at home, in the marketplace, at the basilica. Indoors, outdoors — it made no difference! I had hoped that coming out here to all this fresh air and open sky would offer me some respite. But no: the stench of burning still torments me.' She sniffed the air a moment. 'Can you smell it, too?'

'Can't say that I can, Mother,' Mercutio answered indifferently.

'Well, they say that alcohol *dulls* the senses. Which brings me to the reason why I sent for you. Shall we discuss it over lunch?'

Mercutio knew a rhetorical question when he heard one, or else he would have answered, *Do you mind if we don't?*

Donna Marzia conducted him to a small table by the window, which had been set for them to dine, and they took opposing seats. *Two Dante chairs*, he noted. *So uncomfortable to sit in. Impossible to slouch!*

His mother seated herself with the solemnity of a queen giving audience. She gave the little bell on the table a terse flick of her wrist, and Audrina the kitchen maid entered with their meal. She was quick to lay it out for them, Mercutio noticed, as though she knew there were matters waiting to be discussed and that she would not be thanked, today, for lingering. Apparently, the gravity of this audience was understood far and wide!

Once she'd withdrawn, Mercutio and his mother began a lunch of marble trout, boiled greens and quail's eggs. There was also a pottage of onions and lentils, which he did not look at twice: for it reminded him all too vividly of something he'd seen sliding down a wall in Veronetta.

He shivered.

'Should I send for someone to light the fire, perhaps?' he suggested.

'No,' his mother answered. 'No fires. And I have instructed Glauco there are to be no bonfires on the estate, while I am here. Eat your food and it'll warm you up.'

Mercutio reached for his wine cup, instead, and took a sip. He should have known from the thin colour:

'Surely, it was the Antichrist who turned wine into water?'

Marzia tutted and dropped her fork. Mercutio knew what came next: a roll of the eyes, then a quick prayer said under her breath — *Pardon my son his profane mouth, et cetera, et cetera, Amen* — sealed with a swift sign of the cross. It was something he'd seen her do for him a thousand times before; but he had not expected her to continue the practice now that he was old enough to repent all by himself.

He soon realised his mistake in commenting on the wine, for it gave his mother the appropriate moment to begin her obloquy against his most recent behaviour and general lifestyle. He thought it best to adopt a face of prodigal humility while she reprehended him, though, in truth, he did not take much of it in. He caught the words "reckless" and "dissolute", which he supposed were being condemned; and a mention of "prudence" and "temperance", which were surely being advocated.

'Mother, I know you would not want me to enter a *monastery*,' he said, almost threateningly, 'to become a shadow of who I am. A quiet little man praying and balding in a corner, so that the world does not even know he's there. And posterity shall say, "Oh, what a virtuous fellow! How prudent and temperate he was. He has certainly gone to Heaven. A pity we never knew he existed!"'

'And you think that running amuck with actors and merchants will bring you eternal glory?' Marzia retorted.

'I do not know how you can ever expect me to trust Orazio again,' he said sullenly.

'Actually, I'd say your man exercises a great deal of discre-

203

tion on your behalf, for the most part. Surprising, considering I'm the one paying his wages! You should count yourself lucky to have him. His first and foremost loyalty is always to you. Which is as it should be, I suppose. Better that than a servant who would sell my son's secrets to anyone, for a price.'

Mercutio thought of his valet, sobbing quietly as he cradled him, naked and half-drowned. He had saved his life that very morning, and Mercutio was still not sure if he was thankful. He was sure that Orazio only ever sought to protect him, though, and that he would forgive him for snitching.

What was his mother saying, now? Something about keeping away from places — as well as *persons* — of ill repute. He couldn't claim to be entirely sure who or what was being referred to, but he thought he'd better have a go at justifying himself, nonetheless.

'The Bonifatis might be commoners — maybe even social adventurers — but I'd hardly deem them "persons of ill repute", Mother. Their house was rather wonderful — full of wonders, actually — but I didn't buy anything or sign any contracts.'

'Firstly, I would like to say that one need not attend *every* social event one is invited to,' Marzia replied. 'One uses discretion to determine what may be accepted and what should be declined. Secondly, one is not required to consort with unsavoury characters simply because one has the misfortune to attend the same event. One uses discretion, there, as well.'

'Ah … By "unsavoury characters", I presume you mean the Urbanas?'

'I *do* mean the Urbanas!' Marzia flared, and it was only then that Mercutio realised how angry his mother was. 'Dionigi Urbana and his strumpet of a cousin are a shame to their family and a disgrace to this city! I cannot think *why* my brother, the Prince, saw fit to send them with you to Venice. You might never have formed an attachment to them, if it had not been for the time you spent together on that trip. Oh, when I think of my son taking up with the likes of them? That Pluto and Proserpina! That king and queen of the damned! Oh, I could weep.'

'Oh, Mother, you mustn't do that,' Mercutio entreated, thinking of his father. 'Honestly, I have no attachment to Di-o-what's-his-name and his cousin, Thingy. I can't even remember their names, see? You know it is Romeo and Benvolio Montecchi who are the companions of my bosom. And we are as thick today as … ever we were.'

'How is dear Benvolietto?' Marzia asked, her tone softening.

'He's well. Though you cannot call him "Benvolietto" any more. He is nearly as tall as me, now!'

'He's always been a good boy. Polite. Obedient. And how fares Romeo?'

'Romeo? He's well. Romeo is Romeo …' He'd tried to conceal the pain with which the words left his lips. He was not sure he'd succeeded.

'It is a wonder he has not yet begotten a child, the way he carries on!'

'Romeo is not so reckless.'

'*No*, indeed?'

'He follows his heart, not his loins.'

'I am surprised he has any heart left, the way he gives it away! One girl after another — and, always, *this* one is the love of his life. Baker's daughters, novices and heiresses! Who is it, this time? Rosalina Capuleti, I heard.'

'Her cow-eyed cousin.'

'What, Old Orlando's girl? But I thought she only debuted

in society, this week. Your friend wastes no time, I must say! Though, by all accounts, she is a delightful little creature. Not a *great* beauty, perhaps — not like her mother, at any rate — but they say she has a freshness about her and a natural radiance that is most lovely. They also say she is as pure as the virgin snow. A rarity in these times, to be sure! What a comfort it must be to her mother to have a *virtuous* child.'

'Indeed.'

'Still, proverbial snows have a habit of melting overnight, wherever Romeo Montecchi roams. Then again, one shouldn't overlook the likelihood that it's just another flash in Cupid's pan. It likely will not last the week!'

For once, Mother, you are wrong, when I so wish you were right.

'And what of the terrible feud between their houses?' Marzia went on. 'Riots and duels, servants bloodied in the streets. Hardly conducive to everlasting love! Why, they'd never be permitted to marry —'

'Pottage!'

Silence.

'I beg your pardon?' Marzia asked coolly.

'My pottage,' Mercutio explained innocently, reaching for his bowl. 'Nearly forgot all about it. Don't want it going cold, now, do we? Won't be good for aught but plastering walls, if that happens ...'

He tried to improve his credibility by shovelling several spoonfuls into his mouth, which he immediately regretted. It was not so much the flavour that his pharynx braced itself against, but the sloppy, lumpy texture and the image of that soiled wall in Veronetta. Still, he could hardly spit it back into the bowl — not in front of Mother.

'Speaking of matrimony,' Marzia began, 'I have had another letter from Rome.'

'The *Pope*?'

'No, Mercutio, the Mancini. Enrico Mancini sends his best wishes to your royal uncle, and hopes he may have reason to make his better acquaintance, hereafter.'

'I am sure we shall all be better acquainted in the Hereafter, Mother.'

Another tut. Another sign of the cross.

'He also enquires after you,' she continued, 'and hopes that you are in good health. So kind of him to think of you! He informs me there is a portrait recently completed of his daughter, and wonders if there might be good cause to have it sent to Verona ...'

'Not Porzia Mancini, again!' Mercutio whined like a child.

'Mercutio, Porzia Mancini is *perfect* for you. She is beautiful, kind, graceful, modest, rich, well-bred, well-educated, well-connected. She will bear you children that even the painters of Florence could never hope to do justice! And, most importantly, she is wise. Wise enough to appreciate that all men have private lives, and that a good wife's duties need not include prying into them. Or their nature.'

Mercutio had been rolling his eyes; but he looked at her suddenly. Could she really be saying what it sounded like?

'You see, my son,' she said mildly, 'you may doubt it, but I always have your best interests at heart.'

They did not speak again for a time, and Mercutio chewed over all his mother had said and not quite said. Marzia rang for Audrina, and the girl came to clear the table and bring them a platter of sun-dried fruit and nuts. Mercutio reached for a dried

209

fig, then thought better of it. *For Jesu himself did curse a fig tree for bearing naught but leaves.* He popped an apricot into his mouth instead, and ruminated. Might the day come when a marriage of convenience was in any way palatable to him, for the sake of duty and siring children? He could not deny that his relationship with Angelino had awoken paternal instincts in him, which he'd not known he possessed. Would it not feel the same — better, even — with sons and daughters of his own?

'Might I ask,' he said presently, 'why you are so convinced that marriage will solve all my troubles, when it has hardly been a blessing to my poor brother?'

Mercutio loved his brother. But there had always been a distance between them, even as children. Valentino had been born first, but it was Mercutio who was the golden child their parents had always longed for. Valentino had been a quiet, reserved and sickly boy, whereas Mercutio had been healthy, good-looking, and full of the joys of spring. Marzia did little to disguise the fact that he was her favourite, and Valentino often became an afterthought. When Salvatrice Panzavecchia had once complimented her on her fair sons, Marzia had replied:

'Valentino, fair? Of complexion, perhaps, but his features

have always been so wretchedly plain. My Mercutio, on the other hand, could serve any artist as a model for the Boy Christ.'

Naturally, Mercutio had revelled in such favour as a child. But, as he grew older, he came to see how Valentino was deprived, and it saddled him with a serious sense of guilt. He had tried to reconnect with his brother as a teenager, but Valentino had left home at nineteen to marry and live in a house of his own. Mercutio had seen him rarely thereafter, and they were now virtual strangers.

Valentino had not found married life any more gratifying. His wife was a daughter of the ruling house of Padua, one Caterina da Carrara, whom he first met the week before their wedding. They had been married six years now, but were childless to that day, having endured several miscarriages, stillbirths and bitter fall outs. They remained living in the same house, but were more or less estranged.

'Did he not do everything right?' Mercutio asked. 'Follow every convention? Fulfil all obligations? Yet, I do not think there is an unhappier fellow in all Verona.'

'Who could have foreseen that Valentino's bride would prove to be so shrewish a wife,' Marzia answered, 'or that he would fail to tame her? Or that her womb would discard every blessed child he put into it? That, I believe, is the fount of all their woes.'

'The fault may not be hers,' Mercutio countered.

'*Infertilità* has never troubled our family before. You, yourself, are the last of seven children I bore your father — though it pleased God to take all but you and Valentino to kingdom come.'

'Was it God? I thought it was plague and consumption.'

Marzia tutted and Mercutio crossed himself, this time; a gesture for the departed siblings he'd never known.

'I had hoped that Valentino and Caterina's grief might at least soften their hearts to each other,' he said.

'One would hope,' Marzia replied. 'Though, I suppose it never helps when third parties become involved.'

'Whatever do you mean?' Mercutio asked, knowing full well that his mother meant adultery.

'During Eastertide, it was,' she explained, 'I received some troubling news from a maid in Caterina's service. She told me she had been sent to Valentino's quarters with a message from her mistress, but that he would not admit her. Ultimately, Cater-

212

ina went to deliver the message herself, and she caught a young lady leaving Valentino's bedchamber. Weeks of quarrelling followed! I see you are surprised …'

'Well … I would not have imagined that of Valentino.'

'But I believe you are acquainted with the young lady concerned. Marcantonio di Villafranca's daughter. *La bella* Melania? Though, I suppose you have no attachment to her, either?'

Mercutio did not let his mother see his dismay. Would Melania be so sly with him? With his own *brother*? He would not mention it now, but he recalled that she had boasted to him of a fling she'd had with a wealthy married man, who had bought her some fine Venetian silks and the pearl necklace she'd worn to the Capulets' ball. Had she not even jested that her "old flame" bore a passing resemblance to Mercutio? The thought made his cheeks burn and his forehead prickle. His brother was clearly a deeply unhappy man, and Mercutio knew Melania well enough to know that she had simply been taking advantage.

'None,' he answered his mother tersely.

'I am glad to hear it,' said Marzia. 'Why on earth *signor* Marcantonio allowed that girl to become as big a whore as her mother, I'll never understand. It is Verona's worst-kept secret that Marianne de Bullens was once a courtesan at the French Court, who used her beauty and *charms* to hook herself a rich Veronese husband. But it seems her daughter's ambitions are grander, still. You do know she was shooting her arrows at Count Paride, not so long ago?'

'A harmless flirtation, I'd thought.'

'He proposed to her, last Christmas! His mother, the Dowager Countess, travelled all the way from Lodrone to impress upon him her exception to such a match. Paride gave her up, soon enough; but they say he's been avoiding the Changer of Hearts, ever since.'

'How disappointing for her to miss out on becoming *la contessa*.'

'Oh, I doubt that scheming she-wolf has forgone her ambitions, there. There'll be other men with other titles.'

'Mind how you speak of her, then. You may be curtseying to her as Princess Consort of Verona, one day!'

'I'm glad to say I doubt *that*, even more.'

'Uncle Escalo has been a widower these last ten years. Do

214

you suppose he will ever remarry?'

'I cannot see it happening, now. Perhaps, if he had wed again as soon as the mourning period for his wife and child had ended. But my brother has languished in widowerhood too long, I fear, and he is young no more.'

'So, what will happen to Verona, after him?'

'Word at the Palazzo Grande is that Escalo has mooted a union between Verona and the Republic of Venice.'

'Never! Is that even possible? And how do you know this? Do not tell me you have spies in the royal household, too!'

'Paolina is not a spy! She is a childhood friend of mine who happens to serve at the palace. And who happens to tell me things, now and then.

'Escalo has always thought of you as the closest thing to a son. Valentino, too, for that matter, though I suspect he, like the rest of Verona, prefers you to your brother. Oh, if only I had been half as bold as those great women of old, I would have worked to secure *you* as his heir. My son, the next Prince of Verona.'

Mercutio smiled at her askance.

215

'You doubt a mother's power?' she asked. 'Tell me, how far would Alexander have got if Olympias had not cleared the way for him, first? Would miserable Tiberius have ever been hailed *Caesar* if not for Livia's manoeuvrings? And what of the brat, Nero? Did he not also have his mother to thank?'

'I believe he did so. With a sword! Mother, I did not know you'd read Plutarch. I'm astonished to hear you admire a bunch of ancient pagans, so. After all, they're burning in Dante's first circle of hell, now, aren't they? But, if heathen practices do not offend you, why not emulate the Cleopatras of old Egypt? Marry your brother, murder your sisters, and give birth to your own cousins! Then, you could take the throne all for yourself, with little need of little me.'

Marzia crossed herself against the notion.

'Perhaps I could have got you the throne,' she said. 'But then I ask myself, what would you have done with it? Played with it! Toyed with it! Danced a merry jig around it and never properly sat on the thing, till it was usurped from under you.'

'Maybe I'll surprise you, one day.'

'You have surprised me *every* day, since you were born.' Marzia smiled to herself. 'You know, I called you Diodato for the first year of your life. You were my "Gift from God" …'

'Or "God's Gift",' Mercutio quipped.

'But your father insisted on christening you "Mercutio". I still don't know what it's supposed to mean! A tribute to the planet Mercury? Or the liquid metal, perhaps? You know, he believed that drinking mercury could help him to live forever. Foolish man! I do miss him, so …'

Marzia looked down at her wedding ring. Soon, Mercutio's hand was on it, pressing hers. He found it hard not to think of his father as having already died.

Gian Arturo Marchesino had always been fascinated by science. So much so that he had gone to Padua as a young man to study natural philosophy at the University. Over the subsequent years, he'd slipped deeper and deeper into the world of astronomy and alchemy, fixating on the concepts of an elixir of life and a panacea that could cure all diseases. Marriage and fatherhood proved minor distractions from his life's research, which often took him away from home and travelling around Europe. However, years of experimenting with chemical elements — particularly mercury and its effects on the human body — saw his physical and mental health deteriorate gradually.

Four years ago, he'd fallen ill during a pilgrimage to the Holy Land, where he had hoped to consult with Eastern scientists. He'd been taken to a Greek monastery near Tyre in Lebanon, and he remained in their hospice, to that very day. *Donna Marzia* sent money to the order regularly and received reports on his condition, but he remained too weak to travel home.

Suddenly, Mercutio remembered why he'd been so keen to move out of the Palazzo Marchesino and into lodgings of his own. It was not just the strictness of home — but all the sadness — that had threatened to overwhelm him, that he'd had to get away from.

Clearing his throat, he said, 'The shadows are lengthening. They'll be putting up the chain against those dastardly Milanese, before long.'

'It is not so late,' Marzia said compulsively. 'Must you go? You could always stay the night here and ride back, tomorrow. Anselma can make up a room for you and your page.'

Mercutio shook his head. 'Angelino has lessons with Friar Giovanni, this afternoon. And I am pledged to dine with Benvolio's family, come eventide. We must leave now, or we shall come too late.'

'I fear, too early,' Marzia said quietly. 'For my mind misgives some consequence —'

'Yet hanging in the stars? There are no stars out now, Mother. Only the glorious sun.'

As Mercutio rose from his chair, his eye happened to pass the fireplace. In a mural free of tapestries, he spied the most radiant toddler, who was being ushered along gently by the figure of Saint Zeno, patron of Verona and of children learning to speak and walk. The shining child struck Mercutio as so blessed — so at peace — its hair so fair that, in the painted glare of the sun, it practically became light itself. Then, it occurred to him: was that not the image his mother had been viewing when he'd first entered?

'Is that really me, Mother?' he asked. 'I mean, did I ever really glow … like that?'

Marzia remembered the days it had taken for the artist to sketch her boy, then the months to paint the mural. She wanted to throw her arms around Mercutio now and press him to her, as she had done back then, and tell him how she still loved him so. But she did not, for fear that he would only laugh at her.

You will never truly understand, her heart whispered to him,

219

that in a world where my greatest achievement was the bearing of children, you are my masterpiece.

XVII

Too Great Oppression for a Tender Thing

ERCUTIO left his mother with the agreement that she may inform the Mancini family that they might send a certain portrait to the Palazzo Grande in Verona. He did not go as far as agreeing to view it once it had arrived, but the concession was so historic that it was enough.

Outside, he found his page waiting in the forecourt, petting a red tabby cat.

'I see you're paying you're respects to old Santiago,' Mercutio observed. 'Best mouser in the province.'

'That's thanks to these,' Angelino explained, carefully lifting one of the cat's paws and squeezing the pads gently. 'See how the claws extend and retract? Their feet have the same, but they're usually blunter because of all the climbing they do. When they catch a mouse or rat, they hold it in a fast embrace and use their feet to rake out its innards!'

Santiago seemed pleased with this erudite description of his abilities, and rolled seductively onto his back. Angelino could not resist stroking his soft underbelly, and that was the moment wily Santiago seized onto his arm.

'It's all right, Angelino, don't panic,' said Mercutio. 'He's playing with you, that's all. If you pull away, he'll only dig in deeper.'

'What should I do, *signor* Mercutio?' asked the boy as the cat began gnawing on his fingers.

'Try to relax. Show him he's won — that there's no fight to be had.'

Angelino did as he was counselled, and the cat soon released its grip and kicked his hand away.

'Fie on you, Iago! Begone!' Mercutio barked, and the cat sprang to its feet and bolted away. 'Fly back to Anselma's frigid tit! Angelino, never repeat what I just said in front of your parents. Are you hurt?'

'There's no blood,' the boy replied, inspecting his arm.

'Where are the horses?'

'In the stable, *signore*.'

'And where's my "sweet and juicy something" from the orchards? I am in need of it after the mound of humble pie I just swallowed.'

'My mother makes me eat deer testicles,' Angelino shared as he delved into his pocket, 'for virility.' Withdrawing a fistful of handkerchief, he unwrapped and then presented Mercutio with a shiny lemon.

Mercutio stared at the fruit, and then at his page. 'It is lemon.'

The boy nodded avidly.

'What am I supposed to do with a lemon, Angelino?'

'Well, *signor* Glauco says his lemons are so sweet that you can eat them like oranges.'

'Firstly, do not call him "*signor*". He is a servant — and your mother would have a fit if she heard you! Secondly, did it not occur to you that he might have been pulling your leg?'

The boy thought for a moment, and Mercutio watched his point dawn on him, his little face evolving from one of confusion and reasoning to understanding and shame.

'Well, only one way to find out,' Mercutio said heartily. 'Fetch me my knife.'

Angelino retrieved the hunting knife from Paride's saddlebag, and Mercutio cut the lemon in two. They both took half, and, face to face, eye to eye, they bit into them.

'Where is the villain, now?' Mercutio asked.

'In the dovecote, tending the pigeons,' Angelino spluttered.

'May a flighty dove cack in his eye and save me the bother! Again, do not repeat that. Let's go.'

Tossing their lemon halves to the ground, they mounted their horses and took to the road. Mercutio's exhaustive colloquy with his mother had left his head bursting with as many thoughts as crops in the fields. To provide distraction, he had Angelino recite passages from the works of Geoffrey of Monmouth and Chrétien de Troyes, which the boy had been studying of late with Friar Giovanni.

224

Mercutio remembered when he and Romeo had first discovered the legends of King Arthur. As boys, they had become obsessed after seeing the stories adapted into a fabulous morality play, which had been staged in the Piazza Bra as part of Verona's Easter pageantry. It was all they had talked of for weeks after, and Mercutio had ransacked Prince Escalo's library to find them copies of Chrétien's poems and Geoffrey's chronicles. They had often role-played as the characters, too: Romeo and Benvolio taking such parts as Lancelot and Arthur, while Mercutio had found himself cast in the role of Guinevere. His two friends would battle each other for their lady's hand, and he would reward the victor with kisses. He laughed when he recalled that he had also played the fair Isolde to their Tristan and Mark, as well as the beauteous Igraine to their Uther and Gorlois. Love triangles had been an obligatory part of their play, apparently! Except when they'd quested for the Holy Grail, searching alleyways and churchyards and questioning bemused citizens. He and Romeo had been soulmates, back then. But Romeo had found his Grail now, and things would never be the same.

It was after two o'clock when Mercutio and Angelino arrived back in the city. The watered-down wine at lunch had soothed the itch temporarily; but now the craving was back, and it came with a burning edge, which he attributed to that accursed tincture Dionigi had given him. He was sure it was not the riding that made his muscles ache so, nor the motion that caused his nausea. The sun was hot, but the heat tormenting him came from within. His hair and undershirt were so soaked with sweat that he felt as if he was liquefying! But the sweat turned cold enough to make him shiver, and he could see his hands trembling on the reins. Worst of all, he was becoming irritable, and he wished to part company with his page before he lost his temper. He had only ever lost it with Angelino twice before — and he still regretted both times.

On their way back into the Old Town, they found their way blocked by a riding party. At its head rode a lady, whose horse was led by a squire on foot. Small and pale, the lady was, her long, dark hair plaited and covered with a sheer veil, her brow glinting with a circlet of gold.

'The good time of day to you, *madonna* Ippolita,' Mercutio hailed.

'Good day, *signor* Mercutio,' Angelino's mother returned.

'Your people look equipped for hunting. Is that your pleasure, this afternoon?'

'It will be. I hear my son had a lesson in fencing with *maestro* Teseo, this morning …'

'So he did!'

'But he did not attend.'

'Who needs lessons in building fences?'

'*Signore*, I do not think it needs saying that swordsmanship is a vital skill for any boy destined to lead an army. Angelo is not yet proficient and needs all the guidance and discipline he can get.'

'I dare say you're right, *madonna*. Though the road to knighthood is paved with more than skill at arms. Your son attended me to visit my lady mother, today. He saddled these very steeds you see us upon, before riding like Sir Galahad across eleven miles of countryside! I did present him to my mother at our villa, and he waited on us at table. Indeed, the lady commented on the "chivalry" of his manners. After, he spent an hour or so about the grounds, learning something of husbandry and the running of country estates. Is that not so, boy?'

'Yes, *signor* Mercutio,' Angelino answered.

'Tell us, child, what fertiliser is used in the cultivating of lemon trees?'

'Horse manure, *signor* Mercutio.'

'I couldn't have put it better, myself. You see, *madonna* Ippolita? There is a whole wealth of experiences that may prepare a youth for knighthood. As to fencing, that lesson will be arranged again for the morrow. What Angelo missed today, he'll learn tomorrow.'

'Perhaps Angelo should return to me, for a little while,' Ippolita suggested. 'He can join us on our hunt, and I can make sure he gets to his fencing lesson, tomorrow.'

'I'm sorry, *madonna*, but that would be a great inconvenience to us,' Mercutio replied. 'Angelo has lessons with Friar Giovanni shortly, and I shall need him to valet for me, this evening. Now, we really must hasten about our business, if you'll excuse us. Say goodbye to your mother, Angelino …'

'Goodbye, *madonna*,' the boy chirped.

'Well be with you, gentlemen,' Mercutio said with a touch of his cap to *donna* Ippolita's daughters.

The two sons rode on to the stable-mews and gave their

horses over to Gaspare.

'Marry!' the groom exclaimed. 'Who've *you* got dressed up for? The Pope?'

'The Popess!' Mercutio replied. 'You should know well enough that the Holy Father holds nowhere near as much sway over a man as *she*. For it is she who is mistress of fate, the dealer of destinies, and who must be obeyed above all others!'

'I see,' said Gaspare. 'How is your good mother?'

Mercutio and Angelino walked the short distance to his little house.

'Get changed and then hurry to the friary,' Mercutio instructed him once they were inside. 'Don't forget your books!'

'Yes, sir,' the boy replied, dashing off to his room.

Mercutio went straight to his pantry and retrieved a flagon of wine, which he took directly to his bedchamber. Passing Orazio on the stairs, he exchanged no words, but clapped him on the back: an "all's well" gesture that he hoped was convincing enough.

In the solitude of his room, Mercutio shed his princely

clothes and threw them onto the bed. He uncorked the flagon with his teeth and then drank deeply, trying but failing not to spill it down his chin and onto his linen shirt. Soon, he heard Angelino go out, and he was left feeling utterly alone.

The more he drank, the more annoyed he became. Nobody seemed to care about *his* feelings. What *he* wanted. Everyone was apparently content to let him slowly turn to stone — to become another lovelorn statue, like those of Echo or Orpheus, the memory of their love no more than a shadow haunting deep-set eyes. Did stone beings feel any of the pain etched onto their faces, or recall any part of the stories that shaped them? Perhaps he should go to them, one day, and whisper to each of them the tale of their tears.

It must be a dream …

He was wedded to Porzia Mancini, a lady every bit his equal in beauty and grace. But there was something about him that appeared *changed*. His eyes were glassy, unblinking; his expression mild, inoffensive.

He was sat to dinner with his wife, a vast dining table between them. He gazed at his plate, feeling nothing, unable to find the strength to reach for his fork. His hand was as cold and heavy as marble.

He was stood at the window of his bedchamber, an effigy gazing at the golden moon. Exquisite Porzia was pacing outside the door in her nightdress.

'If you do not love me, then who?' she cried desperately. '*Who*?'

He saw Romeo fading into the darkness, led by a dainty hand.

He saw the stranger in the alley, waiting for him with fire in his eyes.

He saw the round room, where Giacinto and Crisippo and Hylas and Iolaus were assembled and waiting for him. Not forgetting Patroclo — brave, forlorn Patroclo — his kindred spirit, so lost without his Achilles. And there were dozens more youths in dozens more rooms, each one more desirable than the last and available for a price. And in those rooms, Mercutio became flesh again, but his lovers were all stone, their eyes cold, their smiles weak, their voices hollow.

Was that to be his future? Buying intimacy from men who did not care for him? To always taste the indifference on their skin, the resentment in every shallow breath? Mercutio was beautiful; he'd been made to be adored! Such an existence would be bleak. A fate worse than death. A future not worth living for.

XVIII

Do You Bite Your Thumb at Us, Sir?

MERCUTIO woke with a start. Someone was rapping on his bedroom door.

Porzia Mancini?

'*Signor* Mercutio, your friend is here for you,' came Orazio's voice from the other side.

Your friend … Romeo?

He jumped up and rushed downstairs, where he found Benvolio in the hall. His disappointment was momentary, however, as his friend enveloped him in a hearty embrace. He caught the scent of compunction in Benvolio's arms, fresh and bittersweet as herb-grace.

'I met your page, just now,' Benvolio said, 'and he told me you were home. Why did you not send me word that you were riding to Valpolicella? I would have gone with you. Unless … you have not entirely forgiven me, yet?'

'My forgiveness is entirely dependent on you forgiving *me*,' Mercutio assured him. 'And, since I know you are the very soul of forgiveness, you may take your own word for it.'

'Then, I *know* I am forgiven, friend.'

'Unless *you* have not forgiven me,' Mercutio theorised, 'by which token, you will not be forgiving yourself. Perhaps, because you *cannot* forgive yourself. For, if man can forgive himself, what need has he of absolution? But that is a debate for clerics and theologians, is it not?'

'I suppose so, Mercutio …' Benvolio replied, confused.

A sweat had broken on Mercutio's brow. He felt light-headed and stifled, as though the walls of the hallway were closing in on him — as if he were being sealed up in a sepulchre! He closed his eyes.

'I need to get out of here,' he said urgently. 'Will you go with me?'

'Of course,' Benvolio replied. 'The day is still young enough for us to make use of. Though, perhaps you should clean yourself up a bit, first. No offence, my friend, but you look as though the horse you rode to Valpolicella rode *you* back to Verona.'

'Where have you been hiding such wit, all these years?' Mercutio retorted.

He returned to his bedchamber and filled the wash basin with fresh water. Stripping off, he cleaned his body briskly and rinsed his hair. While he dried himself on a linen towel, Benvolio was thoughtful enough to fetch him a clean shirt from his chest of underclothes. Mercutio clambered into a pair of striped hose with leather soles, and then attempted to put the shirt on. He managed to get his head through the opening, but the rest became a struggle; so, Benvolio stepped in to help, patiently guiding his arms through the sleeves, then tying the cords and straightening his cuffs. Mercutio tucked the hem into his hose, before picking a doublet from the trunk by his bed and slipping it on like a jacket.

'Want me to lace it up for you?' Benvolio offered.

'No need,' he replied. 'On a day as hot as today, it'll be cooler wearing it undone. So long as I am not arrested for public in-decency, I am content.'

'There is still every chance of that, Mercutio.'

Finally, he was ready to go.

'Remind me before nightfall that I must go and see Valentino,' he said.

'Oh? And why must you go and see Valentino?'

'To tell him that I love him. I've been thinking about it and, do you know, I am not sure anyone has ever told him that, be-fore? Not in his whole life. Well, perhaps no one else *has* ever loved him, but I do. And so, I will not shrink from telling him.'

'And what will you do when he laughs in your face?'

'Valentino, laugh? You do realise I speak of my *brother*, Valentino? The man has not laughed in five and twenty years! But, perhaps, he will smile. I would like to make him smile, just once, before it is too late.'

'Why too late?'

Mercutio shrugged. 'None of us may live forever. Our time here is shorter than we appreciate.'

'Well, if you have never made your brother smile, then he has never known you. Come, Brother, let us go.'

Mercutio and Benvolio took to the streets. What did it matter that they were narrow and crowded and every bit as rank as his mother had complained, when they were crowned with the open sky, as deep and blue as an ocean?

A leisurely walk along the Porta Borsari avenue brought them to the teeming Piazza delle Erbe. Luckily, they were able to find places at the Madonna Verona fountain to sit and take their ease. The running water offered a coolness of sorts; but it was not long before Mercutio started calling to various people across the piazza: Abramo and Baldassarre, who were running errands for Romeo's parents; Gaspare, who'd been sent to collect some mended bridles from the tanner's, but was dallying a while with his favourite barmaid; Vitale and Ariello Lessini, strumming their lutes outside the Banca Urbana, not so much for coins as for the priceless love of performing; Bardolfo and Ilario, flirting with some ugly fishwives for a discount on Garda salmon.

Mercutio's volume made Benvolio uneasy. He had hoped to keep a low profile today, in light of the recent "troubles". According to Clemenzio, friction between his house and House

Capuleti persisted, despite Prince Escalo's warning. As well as a few minor altercations, there were reports that a scullion at the Palazzo Montecchi had been raped and beaten, last night, by a drunken servant of the Capulets. The citizens of the Watch were investigating the incident; but Benvolio had been told that his cousins, Santino and Graziano, had retaliated already by ambushing a Capulet servant and throwing him into the River Adige.

He feared it would not be long before he was sucked into conflict, himself. When he spotted two strange men across the piazza, he convinced himself they were Capulet scouts, searching for Montecchis to abuse and provoke. They were wearing the traditional colours of House Capuleti, after all: red for blood and yellow for gold, symbols of the family's history as soldiers and mercenaries. The men were soon gone without incident, but it did little to ease Benvolio's mind. He reached for his hip, craving reassurance that his rapier still hung there. The fact that it did only made him feel worse.

'Prithee, Mercutio,' he said presently, 'perhaps we should retire to some cooler, quieter place. The heat is at its zenith — and I swear there are ruffians about.'

'Oh, don't mind Gaspare,' Mercutio replied. 'The only trouble he'll bring is to that wench of his. Not that anyone would notice till she reached full term!'

'I was not thinking of Gaspare, but of the Prince's decree. I'm sure there are Capulets abroad.'

'I wish they *were* abroad. Timbuktu, preferably!'

'And, if we meet them here, there's sure to be some to-do. "For now, these hot days, is the mad blood stirring", as my father often says.'

'He has good cause to caution you so: for *you* are not so innocent when it comes to quarrelling.'

'Whatever do you mean, Mercutio?'

'Precisely this: you are as fiery a fellow as any man in Italy when you're in the right mood — or the wrong mood, as it were.'

'What nonsense! Am I, really?'

'Oho! You'd quarrel with a man for having a hair more or less in his beard than yours — as soon as you've had your first beard, that is! You would wrangle with a fellow for cracking hazelnuts, because it was somehow a slight against your *hazel*

239

eyes.'

'Tush!'

'Did you not scold a man for coughing in the street, because he woke your retrievers as they dozed in the sun?'

'Nooo … Well, if I did it was only because Dane, Scot and Moor were so dog-tired, that day.'

'Did you not also fall out with a tailor for wearing his new doublet before Easter?'

'It is impious to don new fashions until Lent is done. I only told him what any good Christian would have.'

'And did you not quarrel with a cobbler for tying his new shoes with old laces?'

'Mercutio, he was trying to swindle us! Surely you would not have preferred I let his duplicity go unchallenged?'

'I tell you, it is a good job there is but one Benvolio in all Italy. If there were two, there'd soon be none: for both would kill the other!'

'If I were as short-tempered and sharp-tongued as a Mercutio,' Benvolio muttered, 'I could not afford life insurance though

I were richer than Croesus!'

'And, when you have no other to quarrel with, you will sit there and quarrel with yourself! 'Tis self-abuse, my friend. Self-abuse.'

'Self-abuse, indeed!'

They burst out laughing.

That would have been all Benvolio needed to forget his fears and enjoy the rest of the day. If only he hadn't then seen the very thing he'd been dreading. Behind Mercutio, a large company of men was pouring into the piazza, a trooping of red and yellow silk, suede and leather. A sensation like cold water flooded the pit of his stomach: for he knew the man marching at their head, and he had tried to sever his ear the last time they'd met.

Tybalt Capuleti was every bit as fearsome as a lion: tall and strongly built, with sleek hair as black as coal and bright skin as brown as almonds. At his side trotted his cousin, Petruccio, son of Niccolò Capuleti, who appeared forever short and podgy in Tybalt's shadow. Then came sullen Bruto, son of Annibale Capuleti, always preceded by the Greek nose he'd inherited from his Sicilian mother. With him walked Cousin Valenzio, son of

Achille Cattanei and his Capulet wife; the fairest of the pack, inasmuch as his hair and eyes were more honey-coloured than molasses. Then came the same face twice, or so it seemed, for Beronico and Andronico were the twin sons of Orsino Capuleti, a man Mercutio had once branded "unfortunate" to have sired such ugliness in duplicate. Behind them towered the mighty figure of Leonida Capuleti, the eldest of the pack, whose curly hair and curlier beard were iron-grey by thirty. With him was his half-brother, Lisandro, whose rough manners had earned him several wooden teeth over the years, including one from Leonida. There was Druso Capuleti, son of great-uncle Tolomeo and his Florentine wife, who had bestowed their boy with a head of her own flame-coloured hair; and Spartaco Capuleti, sharp and angular as a wolf: he was said to speak but once or twice a year; and Marziale, son of the late Draco Capuleti: he kept his head shaved as a sign of mourning, but had developed a penchant for stroking his fuzzy scalp; and the dashing Vittore, son of Agrippino Capuleti, whose good looks were marred only by a terribly crooked nose, broken in a fall from a horse at the age of six. Trailing him like a pair of dark angels were the last and youngest of the pack, Martello and Tigrotto. The brothers of Fair Rosalina, their chins were even smoother than Benvolio's.

242

'By my head,' Benvolio declared, 'here comes an army of Capulets!'

'By my heel, I care not,' Mercutio returned. Then a wicked mischief brightened his eyes, 'Say, Benvolio, should I ask *signor* Tybalt if it's true that he fucks that beautiful aunt of his while Uncle Orlando lies snoring beside them?'

'I *beg* you, Mercutio, do not!'

Benvolio stood firm as the Capulets surrounded them, pressing his toes into the ground. Mercutio, meanwhile, was determined to show them he didn't give a fig, and had taken off his doublet and begun dunking and rinsing it in the fountain.

'Ah, g'deev'nin', squires,' he said, pretending to have only just noticed them. 'Just getting a spot of washing done. If you'd like to help each other off with your clothes, I'll happily get those done and all!'

His jest was received with scornful sniggers. Tybalt began speaking to him, but he was distracted by Beronico and Andronico, who had taken it upon themselves to introduce Benvolio to their favourite game: surround the target, confuse the target, steal the target's cap. Swift as an arrow, Mercutio put himself between them and his friend, retrieving his cap in the process.

'I can think of better games for twins to play,' he said, passing the cap over his shoulder. 'Ever heard of Soapy Monkey?' Then, he returned his attention to Tybalt:

'My apologies, *signore*. Pray, speak again and I will attend, this time.'

'I *said* we'd like a word with one of you,' Tybalt repeated, his voice dry and rough.

'Which one would that be?' Mercutio enquired.

'The young Montecchi.'

'*All* of you to speak to one of him? He has not that many ears to listen! Nor the voice to answer you, I fear. You see, my friend has been singing in church, all day. Now, he cannot manage so much as a whisper, poor boy.'

'Fine,' Tybalt growled, his maroon eyes glowing in the sun. 'I will ask you. For you consort with Romeo as well, do you not?'

'The gravedigger? I'm afraid not. A little before my time, I should hope!'

'*Montecchi*. You consort with Romeo *Montecchi*.'

'*Con*sort? What am I, his wife? His *whore*?'

There was a favourable mirth from the people on his side of the piazza; so, seeing that the Lessini brothers had their lutes to hand, Mercutio began to sing:

> '*If I was his wife, I'd lead a poor life,*
> *For he spends all night with his whore.*
> *If I was his whore, then I should die poor,*
> *'Cause he fucks all day with his wife!*'

He bowed to the eruption of laughter and applause that followed. However, not one of the Capulets was laughing.

'Gentlemen, please,' said Benvolio, 'let us find some way to peace. Our fair city quakes at every footstep we Montecchi and Capuleti take, dreading the moment one should step upon the other's toes. May we not reason out our grievances like rational men? Or, better yet, may we not simply put them behind us? They surely cannot be so great as to warrant defying Our Lord and Saviour, who did command us "love thy enemies".'

'The Montecchis speak on His behalf, now, do they?' Petruccio Capuleti retorted.

'Get off your high horse!' said Lisandro.

'You'll find it easier to run with both feet on the ground, boy,' added Leonida.

'Perhaps your appeal would've been more effective if you'd sung it,' Mercutio suggested.

'I think, perhaps, we'd better leave,' Benvolio said quietly.

'What, and take a rapier from behind?' Mercutio exclaimed. 'Not I, sirrah! I would rather have it honestly in the chest than up my arse!'

'That is not what is said of you, *signore*,' Petruccio jeered, to the amusement of his kinsmen.

Mercutio did not seem to hear him, however, but had apparently noticed a rough edge to his thumbnail, which he began chewing at.

Petruccio gasped in horror and clutched at Tybalt's arm.

'Do you bite your thumb at us, sir?' Tybalt demanded.

'No, sir, I do bite my thumb *nail*,' Mercutio answered, continuing to do so.

'Well, to the point,' Petruccio snapped. 'Do you bite your thumbnail at *us*, sir?'

'What are you, my nursemaid?' Mercutio cried. 'Quibbling and scolding me for biting my nails! They are my nails, after all, *nonna*! One would think you had caught me sucking my thumb, or had looked down to find me sucking yours!'

'Dost thou suck thy thumb at us, sir?' Gaspare cried out behind him.

Another gale of laughter erupted, blowing through the piazza, against the Capulets.

'Mercutio, you have always favoured the Montecchis over our family,' Marziale Capuleti charged him.

'It is no wonder you side with them in our quarrel, now,' added Druso.

'I take no sides in your petty squabbles,' Mercutio retorted. 'I like where I like and I love where I love. If I have found no love with your family, sirs, then I would have to say that there are more of you than me to blame!'

'Who knows what fallacies and slanders he has repeated to his noble uncle to benefit his Montecchi friends?' said Petruccio.

'Who knows how greatly affection hath made him false!'

Mercutio was about to swear to having exhorted his uncle, that very morning, to have one Petruccio Capuleti fried in his own fat for the sheer fun of it — but, luckily, Valenzio Cattanei intervened:

'Come, now, Cousins,' said the young gallant, 'we go too far.'

'Do we, Cousin?' Tybalt asked sternly.

'True, Mercutio's companions are cut from Montecchi cloth,' Valenzio conceded, 'but that does not make him our foe by default. I, for one, have had some good company from him, which I cannot deny.'

'Valenzio, you do not bear the name of Capuleti,' Petruccio reminded him.

'It is but a minor point, compared to the love we bear thee, Cousin,' Tybalt asserted. 'But, perhaps, in this matter, it makes all the difference.'

Frustrated, Valenzio thought a moment. 'Bruto!' he said suddenly. 'Bruto will attest to what I say. Bruto, when we were lodged at the Doge's Court in Venice, was Mercutio not courteous and amicable with us both, in equal measure, regardless of family name?'

'He was civil,' Bruto answered tersely.

'A damned sight more than can be said of you!' Mercutio exclaimed. 'This surly fellow would not put his lips to mine in the passing of Arabian smoke. So, I blew it in his ear! Even Judas Iscariot was not so proud as to deny his friend a kiss.'

'*Signore*, I am no friend of thine,' said Bruto.

'May such sweet fortune always be mine.'

'Good Mercutio,' Valenzio interjected, 'why are you so hot with us? Despite appearances, we are not thine enemies.'

'True,' Mercutio granted, 'but if the enemy of my enemy is my friend, then the enemies of my friends are *my* enemies. Honest Valenzio, I will tell you plainly that I believe *this* fellow has but one desire, today,' he was pointing squarely at Tybalt, 'murder.'

Tybalt was surprised to be accused so openly, and reacted with exaggerated innocence, eliciting his kinsmen's mockery.

'That cannot be,' said Valenzio. 'Mercutio, you do Tybalt wrong. Who do you suppose he wishes to murder?'

'Mercutio!' cried an ecstatic voice, and they all turned to the Arco della Costa.

XIX

A Plague on Both Your Houses

THERE, beneath the arch where the ancient whale bone hung, stood Romeo. He called out to Mercutio again, his voice filled with joy, and Mercutio knew he'd been missed. But why did Romeo not see the Capulets waiting for him? Why did he run to him, beaming, as though they were the only two in the whole piazza? Mercutio would have swept him up in his arms, there and then, had Tybalt not come between them.

'Peace be with you, Mercutio,' he said, rounding on Romeo. 'Here is my man.'

'I must contest you on that!' Mercutio retorted.

'Romeo,' Tybalt declared, 'the love I bear thee can afford no better term than this: thou art a villain!' With that, he spat on the ground, stunning the whole piazza to silence.

'Quite the ejaculation,' Mercutio said finally. 'Have you been storing that up all day?'

His words triggered a new volley of laughter against the Capulets.

Even Romeo found his lips softening and curving as he answered the insult:

'Tybalt, the reason that I have to love thee doth much excuse the appertaining rage to such a greeting. Villain am I none. Therefore, farewell. I see thou knowest me not.' By those last words, his eyes had returned to Mercutio's.

'Boy,' Tybalt growled, 'this shall not excuse the injuries that thou hast done me. Therefore, turn and draw!'

'I do protest I never injured thee,' Romeo answered, 'but love thee better than thou canst devise, till thou shalt know the reason of my love. And so, good Capulet, which name I tender as dearly as mine own, be satisfied.'

Mercutio could not believe his ears. Romeo was going to turn the other cheek, pardon the public denigration, and speak his reviler fair, even: all for *her*. Did he really think that Tybalt would be as generous once he knew the reason for this good will? Romeo would be the Montecchi seducer who defiled a Capulet virgin and now had legal possession of her. It would be a matter of days before he was found floating in the Adige, the bodies of Paris of Troy and Shechem of Canaan for company.

'O calm, dishonourable, vile submission,' Mercutio railed. '*Alla stoccata* carries it away!' Before Romeo could stop him, he plucked the sword from his friend's scabbard and brandished it aloft. 'Tybalt, you rat-catcher, will you walk?'

'What wouldst thou have with me?' the Capulet replied.

'My wicked way, good King of Cats. But do not fear: I'll take but one of your nine lives!'

'I am for you,' Tybalt answered fatally, drawing his sword with a slow and steady hand.

'Gentle Mercutio, put down my rapier —' Romeo began, but Mercutio raised a hand to silence him.

'Come, sir, your *passado*,' he beckoned Tybalt. 'We are all dying to see it!'

'You *will* be,' Petruccio retorted.

Then it began.

Shouts and cheers rose from the crowd as steel clashed against steel. Mercutio had once been *maestro* Teseo's most promising student; but he was out of practice, and it was not long before Romeo's sword was knocked from his hand. It hit the cobbles with a jarring clang, and he found himself at the point of Tybalt's sword.

'Rule number one: always keep a firm grip,' Tigrotto Capuleti heckled.

Mercutio felt Tybalt's sword-tip press to the naked flesh over his heart. It scraped the golden hairs of his chest like a barber's razor, lingering as Tybalt's gaze lingered. A cruel pleasure burned in his eyes that none but Mercutio could see — perhaps because he had seen it before.

'I think he likes it, Tybalt,' Petruccio jeered.

As Tybalt turned a complacent smile to his cousins, Mercutio seized his chance: he kicked the sword from Tybalt's hand and into the air, cartwheeling away with the fleetness of an acrobat. The Capulets watched in astonishment as he reached up, hardly bothering to look, and caught the sword by the hilt.

'Didn't know I could do *that*, did you?' he said triumphantly. Pointing the sword at Tybalt, he advanced until Romeo's was at his feet. Picking it up, he then tossed the Capulet's back to him.

'Gentlemen, enough!' Romeo pleaded, but neither he, Valenzio nor Benvolio were heeded.

'You know, this is the second time we have crossed swords in four and twenty hours,' said Mercutio.

'What's this, sir?' said Tybalt, stretching his sword arm. 'Ne'er have I fought you, before.'

'No, sir, but I say our *swords* crossed but a night ago. Surely, you have not forgotten?'

Tybalt stared at him a moment, puzzling his words; but he quickly lost patience. 'Sir, you fence more with your tongue than your sword!'

'Ah, so you *do* remember.'

Irritated, yet none the wiser, Tybalt postured himself for a second round, and they duelled again.

The Capulet was concentrating hard now, sweating and grunting with every step, his reflexes tight and brittle. Mercutio, however, remained as cool and fluid as if it were merely a game: and so, Tybalt made mistakes and Mercutio excelled. Frustration drove the Capulet to make a wild lunge at the nimble legs out-stepping him so well, but Mercutio was too quick for him and parried him off-balance. Tybalt stumbled heavily, certain to hit the ground, but Mercutio caught him in his arms. Then, he felt cold steel against his hot throat. He was now Mercutio's hostage.

The Capulets clamoured to free him, but Mercutio warded them off with the point of his sword. Romeo received the same treatment, and the hurt in his eyes was nearly more than Mercutio could bear. But there was no helping it.

Tybalt snatched his chance and twisted free of him. With his liberty came a newfound fury, but not for his captor:

'Romeo! Coward! Will you not fight your own battles? Take back your sword and fight me!'

Romeo was so close that Mercutio was afraid. He was trying to reach him — to calm and reason with him — but Mercutio pushed him away. As far away as possible.

'Stay back,' he warned. 'This is my fight. You'll not shake me off your tail so easily, Cat King!'

He marched towards the Capulets, sword raised, and Tybalt motioned to his cousins to step back.

'You will not rest until you have put my friend in his tomb, will you?' Mercutio demanded.

Tybalt did not answer. The steel in his eyes was answer enough.

They fenced fiercely once more, and by the time they had locked swords, it was Mercutio's eyes that twinkled with mischief.

'May I give you some advice, Prince Tomcat?' he whispered closely. 'The next time you go prowling for strangers in dark alleyways, trim your whiskers better. How my throat still chafes!'

He watched Tybalt's eyes narrow a moment, then ignite with a red flash of understanding. Now, surely, he would rather kill him than Romeo.

Their friends rushed in and pulled them apart. Romeo was shouting something — that the Prince had expressly forbidden such bandying in Verona's streets — but Mercutio barely heard him. The blood was ringing in his ears. The power he'd exerted over Tybalt was more intoxicating than any Saint's Blood tincture. But he knew it would destroy him.

Tybalt struggled desperately to free himself from his cousins. How could it be? That subdued, passive young man at the Palazzo Bonifati — who had yielded to his will so easily — and the brash, wayward Mercutio of House Marchesino: one and the same person! Tybalt needed to face him again — to look into his eyes and know the truth.

'Turn and face me!' he bellowed, charging after him.

Mercutio could not halt the destructive energy fuelling him now, even if he'd wanted to. Taking to his heels, he weaved through the crowd, laughing and singing as he went. Passing the Merchants' Guild, he spotted an old man in a black habit, loitering in the portico.

'Pardon me, Brother,' he said, snatching the monk's psalter from his hand. Then, he turned to confront his pursuer.

Tybalt froze. The veins bulged at his temples and streaked his brow, as though he were swelling with molten rage; but the sight of the holy book seemed to plunge his passion into cold water.

Mercutio flicked through the psalter casually, his eyes

lowered like a saint. Then he took a sudden step forwards.

Tybalt jumped back.

Another step.

Another jump. The sword fell from his hand.

How charming to discover such deep-rooted reverence! It was always surprising, though not uncommon, especially in men with as much to repent as Tybalt Capuleti had. Mercutio wondered just how deeply it ran, so he thrust the book out like a talisman, and Tybalt dropped to his knees. The shot was too perfect to forbear, so Mercutio snapped the psalter shut and dashed it squarely into Tybalt's face, before frolicking away.

Valenzio rushed to Tybalt's side as he climbed back to his feet, wiping the blood from his nose.

'Leave him, Cousin,' Valenzio implored. 'Walk away with me.'

'No!' said Petruccio. 'That clown insults all of us with his insolence! Tybalt will teach him better of it.'

'Tybalt will take his ropery and hang him with it!' Spartaco Capuleti cried.

'Valenzio, would you have it said that your father's star pupil was made into an ass by one of *maestro* Teseo's prancing popinjays?' Vittore Capuleti chimed in.

'He is Prince Escalo's kinsman!' Valenzio returned. 'Harm him and you will pay a terrible price.'

It is only a matter of time before I tell them all how the ferocious Tybalt Capuleti enjoys the taste of men as well as maids, said the masked youth with gilded hair. *What will they say, then?*

Tybalt looked hard into Valenzio's eyes. Then he picked up his sword.

Meanwhile, Mercutio had half-climbed the *aedicula* column at the southern tip of the piazza. Dangling below a marble relief of the Virgin Mary, he waved to the ebullient crowd and blew them kisses. He was particularly attentive to a group of women he saw being led up the Via Cappello by a stout nun. Their shaved heads, bare feet and sackcloth shirts told the world that they were fallen women doing public penance.

'You! Come down from there, at once!' commanded the nun, halting before the column to chastise Mercutio for his impiety. 'Your parents should have thrashed you twice as hard, when you were a child!' However, she had not reckoned on his defi-

260

ance being so contagious, and she nearly collapsed when her penitents began waving back to him, clapping and cheering and flashing their breasts and rears in jubilation.

Mercutio felt as high as if he were dangling from the summit of the Lamberti Tower. Then he felt himself being pulled back down to the ground and into the arms of Romeo and Benvolio.

'I pray thee, Mercutio, fly with us, hence,' Benvolio pleaded.

'I will not budge for no man's pleasure, I!' Mercutio asserted, shaking free of them.

'Why?' Romeo demanded. 'Why are you doing this?'

It looked to Benvolio as though Mercutio leaned in to Romeo's ear, but he did not have time to see properly. 'Here comes Tybalt!' he cried.

Romeo tried to put himself in front of his friend, but Mercutio tussled to push him behind.

'Stay back, Romeo!' he cried desperately.

'I can stop him,' Romeo insisted. 'Hold, Tybalt!'

Mercutio raised his sword.

Tybalt lunged at them, eyes ablaze.

Mercutio couldn't even see the blade till it hit the sun with a blinding flash. He felt the sting in his ribs, sharp as an asp bite. Then it was gone, over, done. For a moment, it was as though nothing had happened; but a scarlet bud began to bloom on the white lawn of his shirt. He reeled, groaning heavily, but Romeo was there to catch him, and they fell to the ground together.

'Come, Tybalt! Away!' cried Petruccio, and the Capulets fled the piazza in a thunder of footfalls.

'A plague on both your houses!' Mercutio cried out. 'Did that mouser get away without a scratch? Let the world see that he runs faster than a panther! Why did you come between us, Romeo? I could not see clearly, for you.'

'I was trying to protect you,' Romeo answered pitifully.

'Hmm … Don't try that again.' Mercutio almost smiled, but he winced sharply.

'Have courage,' Romeo urged, kneeling astride him. 'The wound cannot be so great …' However, the blood-rose continued to bloom relentlessly, and, though he tried and tried, his hands could not stop it.

''Tis not as deep as a well, nor as wide as a crypt's doorway,' said Mercutio, 'but it will see me to mine, just as well.'

'Do not speak so gravely,' Benvolio reproved him.

'I shall be graver tomorrow, I think,' Mercutio replied with a painful chuckle. 'Where is my page? Tell Angelino he was dear to me. Tell him not to weep before his parents.'

'There will be no need of weeping,' Benvolio insisted.

'O, my dear friend,' he said, lifting a finger to catch the jewel glistening on Benvolio's cheek, 'it has already begun.'

The exertion was too much. Mercutio swooned. His blood ran along the cobbles around them, pooling in the hollows.

'No!' Romeo cried, holding him close, trying to give him strength.

Mercutio's grip tightened on his shoulder. 'I love you,' he uttered.

'I love you, too,' Romeo replied, tears welling in his eyes.

Mercutio could have sworn they were made of the bluest opals ... but he mustn't lose focus. He had to make sure Romeo understood.

'I love ... you,' he said again, so lost in those eyes it was as

263

though he was drowning in them. He could no longer breathe. His vision was darkening. There was a fading voice, begging him not to die. The last thing he felt was sweet lips pressing to his, hot tears spilling onto his face. Then, he slipped away.

XX

Fortune's Fool

ROMEO drew back to look. His kiss had not saved him.

'No,' he cried. 'Mercutio, please … Please …'

It was no use. All he could do was cradle the body to him and weep, stroking its curls as one might do for a poorly child.

Benvolio was on his knees, sobbing beside him.

Though it felt unforgivably cruel, the moment finally came when Romeo laid his friend to rest on the ground. As soon as he stepped back, Gaspare came forward to cover the body with his jacket, sniffling quietly.

Not all the Capulets had fled, Romeo saw. Valenzio was still there, white as a ghost. In his arms, he held his young cousins,

Martello and Tigrotto, their faces red with weeping and shame.

'This day's black fate shall darken those to come,' Romeo prophesied. 'The future shall ever be tainted, all joys overshadowed. These salt-tears are but the herald of an ocean, which will crash down on Verona and drown us all in grief.'

'A dark prophecy, Cousin,' said Benvolio. 'Mercutio died, I think, so that you might have your future. Will you toss his gift so readily into the flood?'

'Which way did he go?' Romeo asked absently.

'Who, Cousin?' Benvolio was confused. But, in the second it took to make sense of it, Romeo had snatched up his sword and dashed away.

'No, Romeo!' he cried, racing after him. But he lost him in the crowd.

The Piazza dei Signori was silent, deserted. Prince Escalo was attending a day of meetings between the city council and its legal advisors at the College of Notaries; so, the public had been cleared from the piazza to give them peace.

In the thick shadows along the arcade, Tybalt Capuleti

266

loitered alone. His kinsmen had fled back to their quarter, thinking him with them, but he had broken away to be by himself. He was not sure how he had come to be there — or where *there* was, exactly — but he was glad of the solitude. His heart still pounded like an execution drum. His limbs trembled with unspent energy. His lips were clamped shut, his breaths coming hard and fast through his nose.

He had stabbed people before, but never fatally. He had never seen the life wane in human eyes. When his father, Cesare Capuleti, had died of sepsis many years ago, his mother had shielded him from the worst of it. *Donna* Violante had kept him from visiting his deathbed, and had told him that his father had gone to God sweetly and without pain.

He had seen pain in Mercutio's eyes. Physical pain, of course — but another pain that went beyond that — before they had ever drawn their swords. And what pleasing eyes they had been — he could not deny it — so charming and bright. He remembered them clearly now, framed with a golden mask, glowing like cornflowers in the torchlight.

Tybalt snorted in annoyance. Now was not the time to become distracted! He had to plan what he would do next. Firstly, he needed to get home fast and gather as much money as he could. His aunt, Narcisa, would give him all she had. Then, he would flee the city. He was sure Valenzio would help him. He would go to Cremona, across the border with Lombardy and beyond Prince Escalo's jurisdiction. It was farther to get to than Mantua, but the Capulets had family there. He could rebuild his life with them; maybe even marry one of his cousins.

His future seemed so simple, laid out before him. Yet, his agitation would not abate. The drum in his chest beat on. He started at a flap behind him: just a pair of squabbling pigeons, he discovered, but he felt no relief. There was an angry shout from the street beyond: a petty quarrel or a cry of vengeance, he could not tell. Feet raced upon cobblestones: to the Piazza dei Signori or past it, he could not be sure. He ground his teeth as he watched the southern archway, which led back to the Arco della Costa and the Piazza Erbe. A bead of sweat traced the hard line of his jaw. His eyes detected a faint darkening: a coming shadow. If he was caught now, there would be no escape, no Cremona, no tomorrow. All would be lost, so he must flee.

Turning on his heel, he raced to the piazza's northern exit. The route home was longer that way, but less obvious to anyone looking for him. He'd barely turned the corner to the Church of

Santa Maria Antica, however, when he met a pair of fierce eyes, appearing suddenly before his, burning like blue fire. He felt a sting in his gut, searing and chilling in the same moment. It was only when he pulled away that he saw the dagger, gleaming with his own blood. He fell to the ground and scrambled back the way he came.

'Mercutio's soul is but a little way above our heads,' said Romeo, drawing his sword. 'Either you, or I, or both of us, must go with him.'

'Wretched boy,' Tybalt spat with blood, 'I will make amends to him, yet, by sending you to him, hence.'

Clutching his burning abdomen with one hand, he drew his sword with the other. The sunlight was intense. Black spots speckled his vision like blowflies. The drumbeat filled his ears.

The duel was over in seconds. As soon as the opening came to run Tybalt through, Romeo took it without mercy, thinking only of the merciless death that had been dealt to his friend.

The Capulet was on the ground, but his ox-heart beat on. Rolling onto his belly, he tried to use what blood remained in him to crawl from his desert, but Romeo took out his dagger and fell upon him till he lay still.

The sound of feet pounding cobbles reached a crescendo, and Romeo knew that Benvolio had found him: bloodied, breathless, kneeling beside a body that lay riddled, raw, drained of all life, as Caesar had lain on the Senate floor.

'What have you done?' was all Benvolio could say.

Romeo had never heard his cousin's voice so choked with horror, so appalled and bereft of hope. He had not just slaughtered his enemy, but all his cousin's faith in him. How could he ever be forgiven for doing that? Yet, as he met Benvolio's eye, the dagger falling from his hand, he saw the light dawning. Not forgiveness, necessarily, but compassion, understanding. Perhaps, instead of a monster, Benvolio saw the boy who had been more brother than cousin to him all his life; a boy who'd been broken by the grief he shared.

The first scream came from a window or balcony somewhere above them.

'Cousin, be gone!' Benvolio exhorted. 'The watchmen are coming, and the Prince's troops are on the march. I do not trust you will be spared, if you are taken — so, you must fly! Not home, but to some secret place, where none shall think to look. The cell of the good Friar, perhaps — but go, now!'

Romeo's eyes had fixed on his cousin's pale hands. If he hadn't known better, he would have thought that Benvolio had cut himself. He touched the ferrous-brown stain on his sleeve: the last vestige of Mercutio he would ever see. He'd had his own relics of Mercutio to keep, but they had been lost in the tide of Tybalt's blood.

Benvolio understood all this — without words, he understood — and so, wordlessly, he ripped the sleeve from his forearm and gave it to him.

Romeo folded it carefully and tucked it inside his shirt, against his heart. He would carry it with him as long as he lived.

'O, I am fortune's fool,' he uttered.

A commotion was rising around them. They had been seen, the lurid body at their feet. People were coming. Someone was crying *Murder*!

'Why do you delay?' Benvolio asked desperately, and he tried to push Romeo to running.

Romeo took him by the hands. 'Cousin, promise me that, whatever path you take hereafter, you will always be true to yourself. Find the happiness that was stolen from the rest of us

271

and claim it as your own.'

Benvolio was in no state to make such a promise — indeed, he doubted he would ever know anything like happiness again — but he nodded nonetheless, and they sealed the pledge with a kiss and one final embrace. Then, Romeo turned and hastened to his fate.

EPILOGUE

THE death of Mercutio was the extinguishing of a great light; an eclipse bringing cold and darkness to those who had lived in his radiance. But the ramifications touched even those who had not, for what happened after.

Before the Prince of Verona, the Capulets demanded that Romeo be put to death for the slaying of Tybalt. The Montecchis argued that Romeo's actions had been justified, in light of Mercutio's murder. Tybalt would have surely been executed for his crime, and Romeo had had better cause to exact the sentence than any hangman or headsman. The Capulets insisted that Tybalt had duelled lawfully with Mercutio in defence of his honour, and that Romeo had acted with ignoble savagery, for which he should pay with his life.

Prince Escalo was furious. His decree had been flouted with the direst consequences, and he would punish the culprits dearly, as an example to all. Yet, he could not, in good conscience, condemn Romeo to die. Wrath might very well have driven him to avenge his nephew's death himself, had he been a younger man. And, beyond the unchristian vengeance and brutality of it all, he couldn't help seeing something profoundly human in Romeo's actions. Poetic, even. After all, had Homer not written that Achilles had done the very same when his dear Patroclus was slain by the ruthless Hector? That Romeo and Mercutio had shared a bond as deep and true as the divine heroes of old was a difficult thing to find fault with, let alone punish. Such fierce loyalty between men was admired the world over; a thing to be envied, even. How many could say that he would die for his friend? Kill for his friend? That his friend would kill and die for him?

Bearing that in mind, the Prince ruled that Romeo leave Verona in exile, under pain of death should he return. His heart was hard to Beatrice Montecchi's pleas to pardon her son, for they would be nothing compared to the cries he had yet to hear when his sister learned that her beautiful son was dead.

Donna Marzia did not have time to cry or scream or to contemplate her son's fate, however: within minutes of Anselma breaking the news, she suffered an apoplexy and collapsed.

Romeo's mother lived until the day her son was gone. As

274

darkness fell, she and her husband went to their chapel to pray for his return. *Signor* Federigo retired to bed, but *donna* Beatrice kept her vigil through the night. Come morning, her maids found her on the chapel floor, as cold and forlorn as the idol of the Madonna watching over her.

As for Romeo, he had left the Piazza dei Signori a ghost. Going to the cell of Friar Lorenzo, he flung himself onto the flagstones and wept away the hours. The Friar did his best to comfort him. All was not lost, he assured him. Death commuted to exile was a mercy to be thankful for. Now, he would live to see tomorrow, and his lady love again, and to fight his way back into Fortune's favour.

The Capulets' Nurse said much the same when she joined them, urging Romeo to take heart, for the sake of her young mistress, and to do as the Friar counselled. He should go to Mantua, where he could live quietly until they had found some way to reconcile the Houses of Montecchi and Capuleti, make public his marriage to *donna* Giulietta, convince the Prince to pardon him, and arrange his speedy homecoming. And all Verona would laugh and cheer and sing and dance, once more.

Romeo listened, but did not speak. When all was said, his future had been mapped out for him so thoroughly that it was easier to obey than to think for himself. He would be ruled by them, but his heart did not yield to hope.

Perhaps he would find his hope again in the arms of his lovely bride, the Friar suggested; and so, with the darkening hours, Romeo stole to the Palazzo Capuleti to spend his last night in Verona with the wife he barely knew. The girl lavished him with assurances of her love and wholehearted forgiveness — as well as her virgin body — and Romeo took them all, wanting so desperately for them to be enough. But they were not. Not any more. The wounds inside him were too deep for her to reach, too great for her to even fathom. But she had not known Mercutio. She had not seen what Romeo had done for him.

Rising with the lark, Romeo departed at first light. As he descended her balcony, the girl asked if he thought they would ever meet again. He doubted it not, he answered her gallantly, for it was a miracle that she still nursed some tinder of hope, and he would not snuff it out. But, in his torn and broken heart, he did not believe for a moment that Fortune would be so generous.

Mantua was a fine city. But to Romeo, it was limbo. Everywhere, he saw people just like the ones he'd known in Verona. Bright and merry youths, so like his cousins in their ways. Dear ladies who reminded him so much of his own mother. Yet, he knew none of them. They were all perfect strangers to him, and he was a total alien to them. "The Stranger with the Sleeve", they called him, on account of the colourful keepsake he always wore, incongruous with his otherwise sombre attire, from which they assumed he was in mourning.

The days were hot and humid. The dull sky flashed and rumbled day and night over the city. But there came no rain, no wind, no relief. Romeo spent much of his time reading. He had begun Dante's *Divine Comedy* years ago, but had found no love for *L'Inferno*. Benvolio had admonished him against skipping ahead to *Paradiso*, so he'd left the whole thing unfinished. Yet, now, he felt compelled to pick it up again and throw himself into *Purgatorio*. The epic poem outlined Dante's theory that all sin arises from love: be it the loving of good things to excess, or deficient love that is too weak to compel one to do good, or perverted love that harms and corrupts others.

Romeo pondered the soundness of these assertions. Who was he to gainsay the Supreme Poet of Italy, who had once dined with his great-grandfather at the Palazzo Montecchi? But how

277

could anything as glorious as love be the root of all evil? Love was perfect, despite its imperfections. The one redeeming trait of a race who had killed and enslaved each other for millennia. If a perfect, sinless world required the forgoing of earthly love, who would want to inhabit it? How had mankind convinced itself that that was the ideal world?

Romeo supposed he would find some answers when he advanced to *Paradiso*; but something told him he would not get that far … and he was correct.

One day, among the familiar strangers in the street, he saw a face that was the very likeness of his servant-boy, Baldassarre. Romeo would not believe it, at first, when the boy swore to being the very one, come from Verona to deliver him grave news. In an effort to put the grief of Tybalt's death behind them, the Capulets had expedited Giulietta's marriage to Count Paride, with whom her father had had an understanding. Despairing of what to do, the girl had drunk poison on the eve of her wedding day. Baldassarre had seen her body interred in her family's crypt, that very morning.

That was it, then. It was all over. Romeo thought he should have expected as much. He was not surprised, only certain, now, of what he would do. He would go home to die.

Finally, the skies opened and the rain fell with a vengeance. Sending Baldassarre to fetch his horse, Romeo went to a decrepit little dispensary he'd noted the day he arrived in Mantua. There, he accosted the old proprietor to sell him a poison deadly enough to kill a man with one dose. The poor apothecary yielded, and, for forty ducats, gave him a dram of powder that was guaranteed to do as he desired, twenty times over.

With his death now in his hands, Romeo took to the road. The hard rain had ensured the highway to Verona was all but clear of travellers. Still, night had fallen before he and Baldassarre arrived at the city's gates. The wet and cold had made the Watch lax in their vigilance, and the two slipped by them like ghosts. In the Old Town, they headed to the churchyard where the Capulets kept their family tomb. Romeo parted with his tearful servant at the gates and then entered the grounds.

Verona had not escaped the deluge, and just as the streets flowed like rivers, so did the churchyard ripple like a shallow sea. Romeo waded his way to the chapel's porch, which glimmered with the light of a solitary lantern. The door was locked, and while he looked about for a tool to force it, he was confronted by a pale man bearing a taper. Romeo did not know him in the faint light, but the man recognised him as the young Montecchi lately banished for the killing of Tybalt Capuleti. His return was a breach of the law, the man declared, for which his life was forfeit — to say nothing of trespassing on hallowed ground to rob the tomb of his enemies!

Romeo had not the will to reason with him, only to urge him to leave him to his business and begone. The man would have none of it and sent his page to fetch the Watch; then, he drew his sword and demanded Romeo surrender. Why Romeo fought to live when he meant to die, he did not know, but what followed was a fierce struggle. It ended when they both fell to the ground, for the man struck his head on the wet stone and lay still. Romeo fetched the lantern to see what could be done for him, but his life had flowed away with the rain. He was Count Paride, Mercutio's kinsman and the man to whom Giulietta had been promised. Romeo was sorry for him; they had surely been brothers in grief. Searching his body, he found the iron key on Paride's belt. Now, the door opened for him with a groan of welcome, and he slipped into the silence.

The storm had flooded the chapel, and Romeo found himself wading amongst the pews. Count Paride had prepared an all-night vigil for Giulietta's soul, evidently, for he had lit the chamber with countless candles, even setting lights to float on the floodwater. Following a stream that flowed down a spiralling stair, Romeo descended into the crypt, now a twinkling palace of dim night. The walls glimmered like crystal. Stone angels reached to each other from marble pillars, their hands joined with oil lamps, lighting the way.

The body of Tybalt had been laid to rest on a stone pedestal, dressed with all the pomp of a fallen soldier. Romeo uttered a prayer for his soul as he passed. Their grievance had been settled in this life, and he would not carry it with him into the next one.

There she was, lying on her own pedestal, draped in a gossamer shroud and strewn with flowers. She appeared a sleeping child to his eyes; a maiden of spring, now lost to the Underworld. He drew back the shroud and kissed her. When they had wed, he'd foreseen nothing but joy. When he watched Mercutio die, he knew there could be no more. But she was his wife in the eyes of the law and the eyes of God. She had taken her life because of him. It was only right that he go to his eternal rest beside her.

Looking about, he found a sacramental chalice and dipped it

into the flood. To it, he added the apothecary's powder and drained the chalice in one draught. It was the bitterest taste he'd ever known. Then, he climbed onto the pedestal, lay down beside her and closed his eyes. His head began to swim, as though he were floating on the water below. Lights glittered and sparkled under his eyelids. There came a sensation like fingers caressing his hair; angels easing him into a gentle death. The apothecary had not betrayed him: his drug was fast and true. Hardly able to think, his hand found his right arm and the sleeve marked with the dearest blood. Clutching it to his heart, he died.

He did not live to see the girl's eyes flutter and open, like butterflies emerging from a chrysalis. He did not learn that her death had been a deception, devised by Friar Lorenzo to soften her parents' hearts. He did not hear the Friar come to her now, telling her how desperately their ruse had gone awry. He did not see her take up his dagger — having lost her love, her hope and her honour — and put an end to her life one final time.

Verona was plunged into a dark and lasting grief. The city awoke to unprecedented flooding, and news of the night's terrible events spread like ague. Apparently, Prince Escalo had sent men to bring Giulietta's parents and Romeo's father to the crypt in the early hours. There, they saw for themselves the death and despair their enmity had visited upon their children, and heard the wretched tale of it from Friar Lorenzo, weeping in chains. It was said that Federigo Montecchi and Orlando Capuleti took each other's hands and swore upon the bodies of their son and daughter to bury forever the hatred between their houses.

Six of Verona's noble citizens had gone to their graves within a week, and black drapery hung on every street to mark the loss. Shortly after the mourning period had ended, it was announced that Prince Escalo had taken ill. A few weeks later, the news of his death was broken to the people.

The cataclysm that had claimed Mercutio as its first victim seemed not to have finished with Verona. Less than a year after Prince Escalo's passing, the forces of Gian Galeazzo Visconti marched on the city, and the great chain across the River Adige did not keep them out. Verona was conquered by Milan.

Visconti held the city until his death fifteen years later, when the Carraresi lords of Padua seized their chance to aggrandise. Francesco da Carrara had aided the Milanese invasion, but Visconti had kept none of his promises to share Verona's wealth. With him now dead, Francesco marched into the city, expelled he Milanese, and installed his family as the new rulers of Verona.

The Veronese people loathed the Carraresi even more than the Visconti, and uprisings were a regular occurrence. The Republic of Venice grew wise to the situation and saw an opportunity to expand their own empire. They offered to help the Veronese oust the Carraresi from their city; but, once the deed was done, Verona found itself occupied by the mighty Venetian army. With no alternative, Verona submitted to Venice and became a vassal state of the Serene Republic, losing forever its sovereign independence.

Printed in Great Britain
by Amazon

81227573R00164